ALSO BY JR MILLER

Towers on the Beach (www.towersonthebeach.com)

Now We Are Orphans

A Story of Horror, Hope And Family Love

JR Miller

ARCHWAY
PUBLISHING

Archway Publishing books may be ordered through booksellers or by contacting:

Archway Publishing
1663 Liberty Drive
Bloomington, IN 47403
www.archwaypublishing.com
844-669-3957

ISBN: 978-1-6657-3254-3 (sc)
ISBN: 978-1-6657-3255-0 (e)

Library of Congress Control Number: 2022919868

Print information available on the last page.

Archway Publishing rev. date: 11/26/2022

Introduction

On June 14, 1940, German troops rolled into the streets of Paris from the northwest and marched triumphantly down the famous Avenue des Champs-Élysées in the heart of the French capital. A Frenchman, moved to tears by the image of the Nazi flag with its swastika, could raise his voice only loudly enough for a fellow countryman to hear: "My beautiful country, as we have known it, is no more."

The horrors of war are lived at a very personal level. Some live close to its terror, others at a distance, but all feel its impact on their lives. The brutality of war touches individuals. It rearranges a person's values and character. Orphans of war bear immeasurable emotional and psychological trauma that may last a lifetime.

It is estimated that over ten million European children became war orphans during World War II. Thousands eventually came to the United States. Many were placed in foster care and adopted.

Now We Are Orphans tells the story of how the savagery of war impacted a family living in Lourdes, France. A young French boy and his sister become orphans at the hands of the Nazis after losing their parents. The story follows the boy, Marcel, on his meandering path to adoption, which takes him from France across the Pyrénées Mountains, to orphanages in England and the United States.

This story captures the essence of family love, lost and rediscovered.

Prologue
November, 1992

On this cool, late autumn morning, the sky is pale blue and a flock of Canada geese can be seen flying to their winter destination. The mourners crowd into St. Ignatius Church in Hickory, Maryland. Family and friends greet each other with hugs and tears. They slowly move into the pews of this historic church that was the foundation of Marc Whiteford's faith since his adoption and arrival in Maryland. Several stop to read the obituary from the local newspaper which someone placed on the wall just inside the main entrance.

THE BEL AIR, MARYLAND TIMES NEWS
JOURNAL: FRIDAY, NOVEMBER 20, 1992
OBITUARIES
Marcel Whiteford
Mr. Whiteford, devoted husband, father, and educator, died of complications from a heart attack on November 15 at his home on Eagle Wings Farm.
The Harford County, Maryland resident was 61.
Mr. Marcel Whiteford (Garmon) was a graduate of the Maryland State Teachers College. He received his Master's degree in Education from Loyola College in Baltimore, Maryland. He taught French and English at North Harford High School and

coached the boys' varsity soccer team for over twenty years. He retired in 1991.

He is survived by his wife, Lee; their son, Joseph; his wife, Julie; Marcel's sister, Nicole; and her husband, Lucas. He is predeceased by his adoptive parents, George and Mary Whiteford. A funeral Mass will be held at St. Ignatius Church in Hickory, Maryland at 11:00 a.m. on November 21. He will be buried in the church cemetery.

With no more room in the pews, the mourners line the aisles along the exterior walls of the church and stand shoulder to shoulder in the narthex. Marc's family squeezes into the first pew in front of the altar. The sun makes its way through the stained glass windows as Father Lafferty follows the casket and the six pall bearers. The casket is placed so that Lee can reach out and touch it, keeping Marc close.

The family holds hands. Father Lafferty blesses the casket and whispers to Lee, "Joseph tells me he will deliver Marc's eulogy."

Lee gives a tearful nod.

One
January, 1930

Bon Temps Boulangerie

Lourdes lies near the foothills of the Pyrénées Mountains in southwestern France. In 1858, the town rose to worldwide distinction due to the Marian apparitions seen by the peasant girl, Bernadette Soubirous, who was later canonized by Pope Pius IX in 1862, and veneration of Mary as Our Lady of Lourdes was authorized. The underground spring in the grotto, revealed to Bernadette, was declared to have miraculous qualities, and pilgrims believe that the water has the power to heal.

Lourdes slowly gained prominence as one of the world's well-known sites for religious pilgrimages. Prior to the German invasion of France in 1940, thousands visited the town and the Sanctuary of Our Lady of Lourdes. Yearly, the number of pilgrims increased, and hotels, shops, churches, and homes were built at a rapid pace.

Just two miles from Lourdes is the village of Bartrès, France. It is a small, peaceful place with cobblestone streets and tall, narrow buildings with ivy-coated walls. The village is also well known for its connection to Bernadette Soubirous and is a popular tourist destination.

Claude Garmon was born in this quiet town in 1911. At age fourteen, he met and soon fell in love with Josette Engel. They lived near each other in Bartrès and attended the same primary school in Lourdes. They married in 1930. Their son, Marcel, was born in 1931, and their daughter Nicole arrived in 1934.

A strong Catholic upbringing was provided to Claude by his parents. He loved to hear the stories of the apparitions of the Blessed Mother and visited the grotto frequently with his family. Josette's mother was raised in the Lutheran religion, and her father was Jewish. After she began dating Claude and spending time with his family, she began attending Mass with them.

They were married by a Catholic priest in the garden behind the Lady of Lourdes Church. Soon after the wedding, Josette embraced the Catholic faith. As the years passed, the Garmon family would attend Mass on Sunday and participate in various other religious events. Claude and Josette participated in church activities. Claude assisted with social events and Josette sang in the choir. Marcel became an altar boy and Nicole joined her mother as a member of the children's choir. They were a close, loving family.

Soon after completing his secondary education and marrying Josette, Claude began working in a *boulangerie* (bakery) in Lourdes. The *Bon Temps Boulangerie* (Good Time Bakery), located on the busy *Rue de la Grotto* (Grotto Street), supplied bakery items for many of the hotels. The bakery was old but inviting. The peeling, whitewashed walls displayed many Claude Monet reproductions. There were copper and cast iron pots and pans hanging everywhere. At the back of the shop, two large doors led to a beautiful garden with flowers and herbs. Rosemary, lavender, and thyme, tied with ribbon in small bunches, hung under the front windows. When in bloom, wildflowers sat in a large glass vase in front of the cash register. Daily, Claude and the other employees baked and delivered an assortment of fresh breads and pastries from the oven. They also were busy with walk-in customers who sat at the few tables and booths where they could enjoy a coffee and éclair while discussing world events and the beauty of the shrine. During the warmer months, other small tables were placed on the cobblestone walk in front of the entrance to accommodate the many tourists.

Claude began working there as the clean-up and delivery person, but quickly gained the skills necessary to become the apprentice *pain* (bread) baker. He soon perfected the "cold-dough" baguette, along with artisan and classic breads, croissants and flatbreads. He also created his personal recipe for spice honey bread. The Roman crusaders brought their aromatic spice bread to France in the second century, and it became a favorite in Lourdes. Claude's recipe included rye flour, honey, and aromatic mixed spices. It was one of the bakery's best sellers—fragrant and flavorful.

In a short period of time Claude assumed more responsibility. The elderly owners, Pierre and Lucinda Rabete, liked and trusted his family and him. Lucinda slowly began to educate him on the business part of the bakery. She once asked Claude, "You make excellent bread in the oven, but can you make a profit from the cash register?" Claude worked long hours and usually six days a week. He was told that he was one of the youngest bakers in Lourdes. His love was baking, not the financial side of the business.

As Pierre grew older, he realized that due to some major health issues impacting Lucinda and him, he needed to develop a backup staff of skilled bakers. This would allow him to spend less time at the oven and more time helping Lucinda on the business and marketing side of the boulangerie.

During the years 1935 to 1938, Lourdes was crowded with religious pilgrims and now had almost as many hotels and inns as Paris. Pierre and Lucinda decided it was time to hire some additional help. Pierre knew many of the nearby concierge staff at several hotels. He inquired regarding his need for an experienced baker.

He was promptly introduced to a new arrival to Lourdes who had baking experience. Diop Medar immigrated to France from Cameroon, Africa. At the time, it was a French territory, and due to social and religious unrest, many emigrated from Cameroon to France. Diop lived with his parents in Paris before moving to Lourdes. He spoke excellent French and had never married. He lived in a small room in the basement of one of the nearby hotels and waited tables in the hotel restaurant. After a long conversation one evening at the bakery, Pierre offered Diop a job. Over time, Claude and Diop developed a close friendship. Diop, an excellent rugby and soccer player, would play on the field outside of town with Claude and other young men.

On a busy spring Saturday morning in 1938, as Claude and Diop were removing the croissants from the oven, Pierre caught Claude's eye and motioned him to come closer. *"Un moment, s'il vous plait"* (One moment, if you please). He walked Claude toward the back of the bakery near the small storage closet.

"Lucinda and I were thinking of an idea that I would like to discuss with you. Do you think you would consider moving here to the apartment above the bakery? As Lucinda and I age, the stairs are beginning to bother us. We also have the opportunity to move nearby and live with my cousin. His son was just drafted into the French army, so he has the space and it will be an easy walk to here. You know the layout, and the second bedroom will be large enough for Marcel and Nicole. You will also be closer to your church and a few short steps down the stairs to work. Let me know if you and Josette would want to look at it. Also, do you think Josette would consider working a few hours a week at the counter? If you accept my offer, it will have some financial benefits for you. For the time being, let's keep this conversation just between us. You know how quickly rumors spread."

That evening, as Claude and the family gathered for dinner, Claude shared Pierre's discussion with him. "I know we enjoy our house, but living in the apartment above the bakery does have its advantages, and every year the rent here keeps increasing."

Josette showed interest as Claude carefully laid out the pros and cons. "Claude, tell me, how much longer do you think Pierre and Lucinda will continue to operate the bakery?"

"I think both are in their late sixties. So maybe just a few more years, depending on their health, but you never know. Everything could change quickly, especially with the winds of war all around us. Pierre and Lucinda don't have family who would be interested in the business. You know we have talked about the possibility of buying the bakery, if we could work out the financial part with him. Sometimes I think they look at us as family. Josette, if they made an attractive offer, do you think you would be happy owning a bakery?"

Josette swallowed her forkful of salmon. "I don't know about buying the bakery, but moving to the apartment wouldn't change our lives that much. The children will attend the same school and you already work six days a week, so we can just run down the stairs to say *bonjour* (good day) to you. I think I would like working and waiting on customers a few hours a week. Maybe I could display and sell some of my paintings there."

Marcel and Nicole sat quietly and listened intently to the conversation, occasionally kicking each other under the table.

Claude pushed back from the table and looked at the children. "So, how do you two feel about moving to the apartment above the bakery?" Marcel dropped his fork and stared at his father.

"Papa, I don't want to leave Bartrès. All of my friends are here. We have our garden and the pond with my fish. Why do we have to leave?"

Claude understood Marcel's response and tried to explain some of the positives. "Marcel, you know there is a beautiful garden behind the bakery. I think Monsieur Pierre will let us have a small fish pond. Your school will be closer. There is also a large park where we can play soccer and rugby. We will all enjoy the large balcony that looks out at the mountains. I will be working just downstairs, so you will see me more often. *Maman* (Mother) and I think you will quickly adjust, and Nicole and you will be very happy there. We will have more family time together." Nicole had been silent, but Claude coaxed a response. "Nicole, what do you think?" She stared at Marcel with bright blue eyes.

"Will I still have to sleep with Marcel?"

Claude and Josette both laughed and Josette leaned over to touch her hand. "My little one, Papa will make you your own bed so you will not have to sleep with Marcel. Will that make you happy?"

Two
July, 1938

Understanding Diop

ummer found Claude, Josette, Marcel, and Nicole settled in
the apartment above the Bon Temps Boulangerie. School
was back in session and Marcel liked the shorter walk
and being closer to some of his friends. He also was hoping that
Monsieur Pierre would allow Claude to place a small pond in the
garden behind the bakery. He walked at a leisurely pace up the
stone path toward the rear stairs that led to the apartment with his
book bag over his shoulder. As he got closer, he saw Diop kneeling
in the grass behind the gazebo, striking his breast. His father
had introduced him to Diop, but usually they only waved hello.
Diop quickly stood and waved at Marcel. He greeted him with
a "Bonjour, Marcel!" as he wiped his hands on his soiled white
apron. "You caught me saying my afternoon prayers to Allah! How
was your time at school?"

"*Très bon* (very good), *M'sieur* (Mr.) Diop. I like my teacher
and he surprised us today. He said he is going to teach the class
how to play chess and perhaps start a chess club at school. Papa

has been showing me how to play so I know most of the moves. Do you play chess?"

"Yes, I do know the game of chess and would play it with my friends when I lived in Paris. I have a small chess set that I brought with me. Actually, all of the pieces are wood and were hand carved by my grandfather when we lived in Cameroon. Let me know when you would want to play, but remember, I do not like to lose!" Marcel smiled and yelled back as he ran up the stairs, "Me neither!"

Josette and Nicole greeted Marcel with a warm hug. Josette's oil paints and brushes were spread out on the table in the kitchen. Nicole sat watching each stroke while eating an apple from the tree in the garden. Marcel admired the painting. "Maman, another flower painting? Where will you hang it?"

"*Oui* (yes), it will be a new flower that I have not painted before. See the flowers in the vase near the stove? They are the ones I am painting. These are in bloom now and they are growing in the garden. I am sure you have seen them. They are called periwinkle clematis, and I love the blue and purple color! They were all over Monet's garden in Giverny. When I finish it, I am going to display it downstairs. I think the bakery needs a small gallery that greets our customers when they enter!"

Marcel walked over to look at the flowers. "Maman, they are beautiful. You will have to tell me about your visit to Giverny and all about M'sieur Monet. Tell me, when you will finish this?" Josette set the wet brushes in the jar on the *evier* (sink) and carefully moved the painting off the table. "Marcel, I have only begun this and my guess is that it will take me about six more weeks before it is finished. Since I am working in the bakery a few hours a week, I have less time to devote to my painting. Why are you asking?"

Marcel followed her down the hall to her bedroom. "Our school is looking for a volunteer to give eighth-grade students art lessons every Thursday morning. Just wanted to let you know. I have a letter in my book bag which explains it. I know you are really busy."

Josette laid the painting on the bed. "I wish I could, but now is not a good time for me. How did your day go? Anything exciting happening?"

"Maman, I was just talking to Diop. I told him my teacher was going to give the class chess lessons, and he said he knows how to play. I know Diop doesn't go to our church and that he says he prays to Allah. I just saw him kneeling and praying. Is Allah the same as the Lord we pray to?"

Startled, Josette wondered how to answer such a deep question from a seven-year-old. She placed her hand on his shoulder. "Marcel, yes we are Catholic and we believe in God and Jesus, Mother Mary, and the saints. Diop is of another religion. He is Muslim and believes in Allah, who is his God. We have the Bible and the New Testament, and he has his own holy book that he reads. Papa really likes Diop and knows he is a good person. Remember what Jesus told us: Love thy neighbor. That is what must be in the hearts of everyone."

That evening after the children were in bed, Josette made Claude aware of the conversation she had with Marcel concerning Diop. Claude poured Josette a cup of hot tea and looked for his cigarettes. "Marcel has great curiosity and so many questions! Diop told me he tries to pray five times a day to Allah. Pierre had a long conversation with him about his prayer time. He asked him to only pray twice a day while here at work and try not to let anyone see him. Diop is a hard worker and a great baker. I know Pierre is trying to be understanding."

Josette sipped her tea and moved closer to Claude as he relaxed on the sofa. "Marcel said he is going to learn how to play chess after school. His teacher will give instructions and wants to start a chess club. Diop told him he knows the game." Claude inhaled deeply.

"Chess lessons after school will be a waste of time for him. He is learning the game from me. That's my job, not his teacher's. I'd rather Diop show him some soccer and rugby moves."

Josette walked over and turned on the radio. The Paris channel was announcing the day's news. "Today, September 15, 1938, Adolf Hitler met with British Prime Minister Neville Chamberlain to restate his demand that Czechoslovakia yield the Sudetenland, a region of Czechoslovakia with a large German population, to Nazi Germany. Hitler stated, in a rant, that this demand was not negotiable." Josette was wide-eyed. Claude was not surprised.

"The customers were talking about this in the bakery. It is upsetting news. Hitler is a maniac and wants all of Europe. I am sure his next moves will come quickly. So many here in France remember the Great War, and we lost many. There were no tourists in Lourdes, and many shops closed. Pierre told me his brother and several close friends were killed during that conflict. I think we French are hopeful that the Maginot fortifications along our eastern border will afford some protection, but let's pray that it doesn't come to armed conflict."

Claude walked over and turned off the radio. "I have something important to discuss with you. Pierre has offered to sell us the bakery. I took a quick look at the financing and it looks very favorable. We must visit their banker as soon as possible to settle the property and agree to payment terms. They want to retire by the end of this year. He also would like us to keep them on the payroll for the next two years, providing the bakery is generating enough profit. I know we can increase our sales and cut some expenses. Pierre is very wasteful. I know we will be successful! Also, he said you can begin to display your art near the front counter."

Josette touched Claude's hand, pulled him closer, and gave him a warm kiss. "So on January 1, 1939, we will own the Bon

Temps Boulangerie in Lourdes, France. Time to celebrate!" She took a bottle of champagne from the wine rack, handed it to Claude, and found two glasses. Claude poured, and they raised their glasses. With a loving smile, Josette made the toast: "May all of our dreams come true. I am so happy, and thank you for making this happen. I love you!"

Three
February, 1939

Diop's Sickness

On this Saturday morning, the mountain winds did not want to let go of winter. Everyone was bundled up, and the apartment had heating issues. The two wood stoves and small coal furnace in the bakery usually kept the apartment warm, but Claude had not determined why he was having issues with the heat. The children were wearing their coats most of the time. Josette, wrapped in her robe, wool pajamas, and a blanket, walked down the steps to the bakery and motioned to Claude. He walked over with a bag of pastries. "Please take these up to the children. Let them know that I am working on the heat problem." Josette rolled her shoulders.

"Claude, we are so cold. Can't you do something?" Claude tenderly touched her pink cheeks.

"I am waiting for Diop. He has some experience with coal furnaces. I will ask him to take a look as soon as he arrives this morning. We may have to come up to the apartment to check the heat vents. I thought he would be here by now. He is usually here by 7:00 on Saturdays." Josette took the bag and shuffled up the stairs.

Close to noon, Diop haltingly made his way through the back entrance. He hung up his coat and grabbed his apron. Claude could see from his sunken eyes and pale face that Diop was unwell.

"What's wrong Diop? I have been worried about you." Shaking and coughing, Diop sat down in the small chair near the oven. "I was up all night and am having a difficult time breathing. I have chills. I ache all over. I thought I could work, but I must leave. I don't want to pass this germ around." Claude stepped back and handed him his coat.

"Diop, yes, please go back to your room. I will stop by this afternoon and check on you. So sorry you are sick!"

Not long after Diop left, Pierre wandered in for his weekly visit and filled a large bag with some of Claude's spiced honey bread. Claude saw him and waved.

"Bonjour, Pierre." Pierre looked around and walked over.

"You are busy with a crowd of customers, in spite of the weather. Where is Diop? Did you give him the day off?"

Claude placed some croissants in Pierre's bag. "These are for Lucinda. Diop came in, but had to leave. He looked very sick and said he was up all night."

Pierre looked at the cash in the register. He grabbed a few francs and placed them in his pocket.

"Looks like you are having a good day! It sounds like Diop may have the influenza. This is the time of year when it is most contagious. He will need to take some medication. Maybe you should call Dr. Deter?"

Claude handed Pierre an envelope. "This is next month's payment. Pierre, we are having some heating issues in the apartment. Any idea what might be wrong?" Pierre walked toward the back door and motioned to Claude.

"Let's look first at the coal bin out back." They walked outside and Pierre leaned over and felt the coal.

"Claude, you need to keep the coal covered. This coal is wet from all the rain and sleet. That is your problem. It will take some time to dry this load. Contact the coal company and ask for another delivery. Remember, the furnace only likes dry coal."

Later that afternoon, Josette came down to help at the counter and wait on customers. Claude walked over to her with his coat on. "I am going over to the hotel where Diop lives and check on him. I shouldn't be that long." She filled a bag with some sweet rolls.

"Give this to him and tell him we hope he is feeling better. Please don't get close to him. You know how quickly that germ can spread. As soon as you return, take a bath and I will wash your clothes." Claude gave her a thumbs-up as he hurried out the door.

Claude walked quickly down the cobblestone sidewalks along the River Gave de Pau to the Hôtel Albon. He walked up to the front desk and was greeted by Thomas, a frequent bakery customer, wearing the hotel uniform.

"*Bon soir, M'sieur Claude. Comment vas-tu?*" (Good evening, Mister Claude. How are you?).

"Très bon, Thomas. I would like to check on Diop. He was too sick to work today, so I told him I would stop by to see how he was feeling. I know where his room is. May I go down the back stairs? Perhaps I should take a key just in case he can't come to the door."

Claude walked down the dim, narrow stairs and down the hall to Diop's room. He knocked and waited but there was no response. Finally the door slowly opened. Diop stared at Claude and stumbled over to sit on the side of the bed. Claude stood by the door, a good six feet from Diop. He placed the bag from

Josette on the dresser. "Something from Josette. Are you feeling any better?" Diop moved the pillow and wanted to lie down.

"Actually I am feeling worse. Almost as bad as when I had malaria in Cameroon, and that lasted for weeks. I need some medication. Is there a doctor I can contact? I can't control my bladder and I know I am dehydrated."

Claude moved just a bit closer. "Diop, you can hardly keep your eyes open. I will contact our family doctor."

"*Merci* (thank you), Claude." Claude closed and locked the door and made his way back to the front desk.

"Thomas, Diop is very sick and I would like my doctor to come look at him." Claude found Dr. Deter's number on an old folded note in his wallet as Thomas handed him the phone. "He said he is nearby and will be here soon. Thomas, would you please send him down when he arrives?"

Within the hour there was a knock on Diop's door. Dr. Lucas Deter stood in the doorway with his medicine bag, top coat, and brown Stetson wool fedora pulled down almost covering his eyes. "Claude, so good to see you again. Tell me, what is the urgency with your friend?" Claude pointed to Diop as Dr. Deter took off his coat and hat and opened his bag.

"Doctor Deter, this is one of my bakers who is very sick. It may be influenza, so I wanted you to look at him." Diop opened his eyes and shook with a cough as Dr. Deter took his pulse and listened to his heart. He touched his forehead and felt the high fever. He reached in his bag and removed two face masks and handed one to Claude. He adjusted his to fit tighter around his nose.

"Here Claude, put this on and stand over there. If he does have influenza, it is very contagious."

Dr. Deter asked Diop when he first felt sick. Diop tried to sit up and gave a weak reply. "On Friday I started to feel sick and could hardly get out of bed this morning. I did want to tell you that five years ago, when living in Cameroon, I had malaria. Could it come back to me?" Doctor Deter took his blood pressure and with a concerned look, shook his head.

"Very low and a very weak heart rate. Yes Diop, malaria can return and maybe that is what has happened. It is most likely a combination of issues. We need to get you to the hospital. Claude, can you transport him in your vehicle? I will meet you there."

Dr. Deter returned Claude to the bakery. "I will meet you at the hospital. Bring him to the front entrance. Someone will be waiting for you. I am very worried about Diop. He is a very sick young man. I hope I can find the correct medication for him. He may be at the hospital for some time. I hope he has not passed on the germ to those at the bakery. At the hospital I will give you several thermometers so that your workers can take their temperatures. If anyone's is elevated, send them home immediately."

Claude hurried into the bakery and told Josette what was happening. "I am taking the truck and will drive Diop to the hospital, St. Jean Luc. Dr. Deter will meet us there. I am very worried about him."

Claude arrived at the hotel and asked Thomas if he would help him move Diop to his truck. Claude and Thomas held him tightly under each arm and took him down the hall to the freight elevator. Diop dragged his feet and was semi-conscious, his head jerking from side to side. They placed him in the front seat. Thomas closed the door as Claude pulled away and drove through the narrow streets to the driveway up to the main hospital entrance. As Dr. Deter promised, two nurses were waiting. Claude greeted them as a tall nurse dressed in a blue uniform opened the door. "M'sieur, we will take over from here. There is a waiting room inside the main entrance."

Time crawled as Claude paced the floor in the small waiting room. Dr. Deter finally walked in and motioned Claude to sit on the wooden chair. "Claude, he is not doing well. We are treating him for influenza, but I do believe his malaria is back, which complicates his prognosis but is not unusual. We call it the "recurrence." The malaria parasite has been dormant inside his liver, but now it has resurfaced. I am afraid he has now drifted into a coma. The doctors here will be with him throughout the night. Prayers will help more than medication. I have to go, but I will contact you tomorrow."

It was close to 4 a.m. when Claude made his way up the back stairs of the apartment. He inserted his key, entered the kitchen, and was surprised to see a candle burning on the table and Josette sipping her tea. Her eyes were tired and her face was drawn with worry. "I am so concerned about Diop. What is Dr. Deter telling you? It must be serious for you to be this late!"

Claude explained everything Dr. Deter had told him. "He said he is in a coma. I don't think he is going to make it. I know it's late, but let's try to attend the 9:00 Mass this morning. Diop needs our prayers. Father Paul usually conducts the service and he knows Diop. He always stops to talk to him when he comes by the bakery."

Claude, Josette, Marcel, and Nicole sat in their usual place in front of the St. Joseph statue within the spacious Basilica of Our Lady of the Rosary. After Mass, Father Paul stood outside of the church at the top of the steps. Claude and the family walked over to the priest. "Bonjour, Father. Hope you are well," Claude said as he shook the priest's hand. "Father, Diop who works for us is very sick and is now in a coma at St. Jean Luc Hospital. Our family is very worried about him."

Father Paul pulled his scarf tighter around his neck as Claude related all of the medical information that Doctor Deter had given him. Father Paul placed his hand on Nicole's head as she stared up into his brown eyes. "This does not sound good. As soon as I finish here and change I will go see him. I should be there within an hour or so. I will bring some of the Lourdes holy water. Would you like to meet me there?" Claude looked at Josette.

"Father, I can meet you there. Josette needs to get back to the bakery."

Claude said good-bye to the family and took the quick walk to the hospital. He entered the second floor ward of beds, spoke to the nurse, and walked toward Diop. As he placed his mask on his face he saw that Diop was sleeping and his breathing was labored. He stared at the medical devices tethered to him. After a while, Father Paul approached and touched Claude on his shoulder. "Has the doctor given you an update? Any improvement?" Claude and the priest moved away from the bed.

"Thank you for coming. I have not seen the doctor, but the nurse said he is still comatose and he did not have a good night. They think the malaria has returned. I have tried to contact his parents in Paris, but I have not been successful. Father, I guess you know a little about Diop. He was born in Cameroon and his family moved to Paris. He came to Lourdes about two years ago looking for work. He is not Catholic, but a devout Muslim."

Father Paul wrinkled his face at the unexpected comment. "Although he and I have had several conversations, I did not know that he is a Muslim. That is surprising. There are no mosques in Lourdes, so I am sure that has troubled him. Our Lady loves all people regardless of their religion." Father Paul opened a small brown bag and gently removed a bottle of water. "This is water directly from the Lourdes Grotto. We keep a supply at our rectory. It has been blessed by the Bishop. I would like to anoint Diop with this holy water." Father Paul removed the cap and sprinkled the water on Diop's head, lips, and hands, reciting the prayer of healing:

"Holy Mary, by appearing in the Grotto of Lourdes, you were pleased to make it a privileged sanctuary, whence you dispense your favors, and already many sufferers have obtained the cure of their infirmities, both spiritual and corporal. I ask, with the most unbounded confidence, to implore your maternal intercession on behalf of our friend, Diop. May your holy water heal him. O loving Mother, please grant my request."

Claude made the sign of the cross and touched Diop's hand. Diop stirred, but did not open his eyes. Father Paul returned the cap and placed the bottle back in the bag. He shook Claude's hand. "Claude, let us hope that a miracle happens and his health returns. It is in the hands of the Lord. He will be in my prayers. I am in this hospital often, so I will stop by to check on him."

It was late that winter Sunday evening when they both left the hospital and Claude made his way back to the bakery. The mountain winds continued to blow and move the branches on the leafless trees. Claude pulled his hat over his ears and entered the warmth of the bakery. There were a few customers standing in front of the checkout counter. Josette was busy and gave him only a quick wave. Claude took off his coat, found his apron, and began to wait on customers. Soon the last customer left. Claude locked the front door, and with his wife walked up the thirteen steps to their apartment.

Later at dinner, tears blurring his eyes, Claude told Josette and the children that Diop was dying. "If you would have seen him today, you would be saying the same. I must contact his parents in Paris. Maybe Thomas, at the hotel where he has a room, might know how to reach them. Tomorrow I will stop by the hotel on my way to the hospital. Let's pray for him." The four held hands, bowed their heads, and recited a prayer for the sick.

On Monday afternoon, usually a slow day at the bakery, Claude arrived at the hospital to see Dr. Deter standing next to Diop's bed. Claude's first thought was that his friend had passed during the night, but to his surprise Diop was awake and propped up on his pillow. Claude almost shouted in amazement. "Diop, I was not expecting to see you like this! This is such a surprise! Thank you, Lord!"

Dr. Deter looked at Claude. "I agree—this is miraculous. I was expecting the worst and was amazed to see such improvement! The nurse told me that you and Father Paul were here yesterday and that Father anointed Diop with Lourdes water."

With a weak voice, Diop softly replied to Claude. "I did not know. I think your Holy Mother helped me." Dr. Deter handed him a glass of water and several pills.

"Take these. Let's hope you continue to improve. I think the Lourdes water was the miracle you needed."

Four
April, 1939

The War Moves Closer

Diop made a miraculous recovery and returned to work on the first Sunday in April of 1939. Having had long conversations with Father Paul, and believing that his recovery was due to the intersession of Our Lady of Lourdes, Diop carefully studied the Catholic faith and decided to embrace a new religion. He was baptized on Easter Sunday, April 9, 1939. Claude, Josette, Marcel, and Nicole were there, and Father Paul conducted the service. Following the baptism, Diop was invited back to their apartment for dinner.

Everyone was joyous, and Diop wanted to repay them in a small way for their kindness and insisted on cooking dinner. This made Josette very happy. She also liked that Diop was a vegetarian and loved his ratatouille and Roquefort with caramelized onion tart. That afternoon he prepared the ratatouille with eggplant and zucchini along with onions, mushrooms, bell peppers, and tomatoes. Josette was delighted with his presentation. "Diop, this looks delicious. How did you learn to cook like this?" Diop placed the large bowl in the center of the table.

"My father is a cook and my mother, a baker. I guess I was a good student!"

Claude enjoyed the dish. "Très bon, Diop, and welcome to our religion. I wanted to ask about your parents. I tried to contact them in Paris and found a note you had given me with their address. I wanted them to know about your illness. I sent a telegram to that address but received no reply." Diop pulled up his chair.

"They are no longer at that address. I will have to give you their new location. They tell me the political climate in Paris is changing and immigrants are not being treated well. Housing for them has been difficult."

Marcel was playing with his food. He would have preferred rabbit to the ratatouille and moved the food around on his plate as he tried to get Diop's attention. "Papa tells me you are a good soccer player. Do you think we could walk to the park and kick the ball around after we finish our dinner? Papa, will you come with us?" Claude added another spoonful to his plate. "Excellent idea, if Diop has the time and feels up to it. Maybe Maman and Nicole will join us. I will go over ahead of everyone. I have some Easter eggs to hide!" Nicole and Marcel clapped their hands.

After a beautiful warm summer, at the end of August, Claude began to notice that the number of tourists had diminished, leaving empty rooms at many of the hotels and fewer customers in the bakery. Summer was the high season for tourists, mainly religious pilgrims visiting Lourdes, but this year was different. The war was moving closer to Lourdes. Claude noticed a continual slump in sales and began to worry. He and Josette followed the newspapers and learned that Germany was moving closer to war.

On September 1, 1939, speculation ended as Germany invaded Poland, and France responded by declaring war on

Germany on September 3 along with Great Britain, Australia, and New Zealand. Canada entered the war a few weeks later, but not the United States. The world was once again at war.

There were immediate and dramatic changes all over France. All healthy young men were being conscripted into the military. Lourdes was becoming a town of old men, women, and children. One of the young men working for Claude, Henri, left to join the French Army. Stores, apartments, houses, and all residences were required to install black-out curtains. Street lights were turned off and a 9 p.m. curfew was imposed. There were lines at the grocery stores, and rationing began at the bakery.

In late September 1939, Marcel and Nicole came home from school to an empty bakery with Diop standing outside smoking. They waved and hurried past to see Claude and Josette sitting at one of the outdoor tables sipping coffee. Marcel ran to them with Nicole trailing behind. "My teacher has left! Our principal had to teach our class today. They said he was in the French army and will be fighting the Germans. Papa, what does all this talk about war with Germany mean? Why doesn't Germany like France? Will you have to close the bakery? Will you have to join the army? Will our school close?" Marcel opened his book bag and pulled out two gas masks. "This is what they gave us today. Here is one for Nicole."

Claude looked at his beautiful children and wondered if they could understand. "Here, both of you sit so we can have one of our family conversations. Maman and I just received a letter from our mayor and it said that our bakery must remain open because it provides essential needs for the town and the soldiers that are housed here. It said that, for the immediate future, all of the remaining male employees working here are exempt from military service, which means business as usual. Do you understand? The bakery will stay open and our lives should not change that much. You realize that your school is essential, so

I think Nicole and you will be attending the same school, but you may see some changes. So please don't worry. Life here may become different, but our family will be fine! France is at war with Germany, but let's pray it will be brief and we will be safe. If we are steadfast in our prayers, our Blessed Mother will continue to watch over Lourdes and protect us."

Claude and Josette could see that Marcel was processing what he was just told, but Nicole was crying. Josette pulled her close. "Little one, tell me, why are you crying? Does all of this talk frighten you?"

Nicole rested her head on Josette's shoulder. "Maman, today my friend George made fun of my *tache de naissance* (birthmark). He told the class that I had a tattoo on my hand and was teasing me. I tried to hide my hand, but everyone wanted to see it. It made me feel ugly and everyone was laughing at me."

Josette wiped Nicole's tears with her napkin. "Nicole, you are a beautiful little girl, and the mark can hardly be seen. It is just a red dot that sits on top of your finger. Please don't be unhappy about it. Once your classmates satisfy their curiosity, they will not pay any more attention to it. I will walk you to school tomorrow and talk to your teacher about your friend George." Nicole threw her arms around her mother's neck and pulled her close. "Merci, Maman. *Je t'aime*" (I love you).

With France at war, the bakery continued to lose business. Only Claude, Josette, and Diop were working. Many small shops along the main street had closed. The winter of 1939-1940 was one of the coldest on record. Coal was hard to find and electricity was spotty. School was closed between November and March because of the freezing cold temperatures and frozen pipes. Everyone at the bakery wore layers of clothing in spite of the heat from the ovens.

With the bakery downsized due to the economic circumstances, Claude asked Diop if he would be interested in moving from his hotel room to the bakery. He showed Diop the small, mostly-empty storeroom that boasted a large window overlooking the garden. "Diop, we can move everything out of here and move in your bed and dresser. What do you think?" Diop agreed, and within a week he took up residence at the Bon Temps Boulangerie.

The news that Claude and Josette heard from the BBC (British Broadcasting Corp.) was that France was losing the conflict. On May 10, 1940, the Battle of France began in earnest as the German army breached the Maginot Line. On June 3, 1940, Paris was bombed by the German Luftwaffe, and 254 people were killed. Most of the victims were civilians, including schoolchildren. Ninety-seven buildings were destroyed or severely damaged, and sixty-one fires were set by the German planes. The official statement broadcast said that a total of 1,060 bombs fell on the Paris area, eighty-three of them landing on the city of Paris itself. Fires destroyed many of the older historical buildings as well as shops and hotels. This horror sent a clear message throughout France that Germany would continue to decimate the country, wrecking its economy and military with no regard for civilian casualties.

On Monday, June 10, 1940, Josette opened the bakery and Claude began to set out the breads and pastries that Diop and he had been baking since before daybreak. It was a slow weekend with few customers, but two of the nearby hotels continued to buy from them.

Soon after Josette unlocked the door, a tall postal messenger dismounted his bicycle and entered the shop. After looking through his bag and producing a letter, he spoke to Josette. "Madame, have you a Diop Medar living here? This letter is addressed to him." Josette stepped forward.

"Yes we do. Let me find him." Josette located Diop, who approached the messenger.

"I am Diop Medar." The messenger asked for an identity card. Nervous and puzzled, Diop pulled his identification card from his wallet and showed it to him. The messenger handed the letter to him and made a quick exit. Diop tore the envelope open and began to read the contents. Claude and Josette were standing next to him as he began to cry. With hesitation, he raised his head and looked at them. He could hardly speak.

"The letter is from my mother. My father was killed last week during the German air attack on Paris. The hotel where he works was bombed. He died when the roof collapsed on three other workers and him. Mother said there was no need for me to return to Paris. It's too dangerous. She will let me know where his final resting place will be."

Diop suddenly looked as though he were about to collapse. Claude and Josette placed their arms around him. Claude handed him his handkerchief. "Let us walk you back to your room and I will bring you coffee and something to eat. This is such a tragedy for you and so unexpected. We are hurting as well. You told us so many things about your father and your mother. We felt that we knew them."

Later in the afternoon, Marcel and Nicole made their way down the stairs and walked back to Diop's small room. They knocked with gentle taps. When Diop opened the door, they both surrounded him with hugs. Nicole handed him a card she had made. Marcel pointed to it and said, "It is from both of us, and Maman helped!" There was a large heart drawn on the front of the card. Diop read the neat handwritten script.

Diop, please know that we are here for you and you are not alone. We can't imagine how painful and heartbreaking it must be to lose your father in this horrible war. We are here whenever you need us. All our love, Nicole and Marcel.

Five
June, 1940

The Horror of War

The Garmon family watched the war unfold at their doorstep. France had seen several military setbacks. The Maginot Line did not provide the protection as expected. On June 12, 1940, over thirteen thousand French and British troops surrendered to German Field Marshall Erwin Rommel. Just two days later, on June 14, Paris fell under German occupation and French citizens were shaken when they saw German troops goose step past the Arc de Triomphe. The French realized that they had lost the war with Germany, and on June 17 Hitler installed his puppet, Marshal Philippe Pétain, as Prime Minister. On June 22, an armistice was signed, ending the Battle of France.

France was now a divided country with the *Zone Occupé* (Occupied Zone) to the north and west under strict German control and the *Zone Libre* (Free Zone) to the south under the supposed control of Pétain with his headquarters in Vichy, France. Germany occupied the North Sea and the Atlantic coasts of France and their hinterlands. The Vichy regime retained the "unoccupied" territory in the south. Lourdes, located in the High Pyrénées Department, fell within the "Unoccupied Free Zone," controlled by Vichy. The Garmons wondered how long the "Free Zone" would remain free with Pétain and his government kissing Hitler's cheeks.

Claude, Josette, and Diop continued their daily routine, but noticed changes throughout Lourdes. Mail delivery was slow and unreliable. There were long lines in the grocery and butcher shops, and the ration cards only meant fewer goods. Supplies for the bakery were hard to come by.

In early summer they began to hear about the refugees from the Occupied Zone making a mass exodus on the roads to all parts of southern and western France. Thousands walked away from work, homes and family, afraid that the German brutality of World War I would visit them once again. Many found their way to Lourdes on their journey.

Near daybreak on a hot summer morning, Josette and Claude awakened to voices in the garden behind the bakery. Josette grabbed her robe and walked out onto the balcony to find below several families sleeping under the garden pergola, while others helped themselves to the vegetables in her garden. Many were using the garden hose to fill their bottles.

Diop heard the commotion and rushed out to confront the trespassers. He walked over and took the hose from a young father standing next to his wife and small boy. The father tugged on the hose as he looked at Diop with weary eyes.

"Please, Monsieur, surely you will not deny us something to drink? Our group has been on the road for weeks. Some of our children are sick, and we are hungry with no money. Can you help us? We all are French."

Josette and Claude heard their conversation from the balcony. Claude looked at Josette. "Let me go down and gather something to give to them." Claude went down to the bakery and filled several trays of breads and other pastries and took them to the group. Diop helped distribute the surprise breakfast to the gathering crowd. Claude provided a second offering, exhausting his daily inventory. The crowd slowly disbursed as Claude and Diop surveyed the damage and the mess left behind: torn shoes, dirty diapers, papers, and empty boxes. "Diop, don't worry about the mess. We must start baking. I think I have learned my lesson. Lock the garden gate."

On an August morning in 1940, Josette opened the bakery as Claude and Diop placed breads, baguettes and brioche in the ovens. As she opened the door, she saw a paper lying at her feet. She picked it up and read the large type across the top of the page: *THE MAQUIS FOR FRENCH FREEDOM*. There had been talk among her customers about the French Resistance fighters circulating anti-German information and news that wasn't full of German propaganda. She walked back and showed the paper to Claude and Diop. Claude took the paper and read it as Diop looked over his shoulder.

"This is what we have heard about. It states that General de Gaulle is calling on the French people to take up arms and resist the German occupation. He said that Pétain is a false prophet who has sold out the French to German terror. Whoever is distributing this is doing it at great danger. If they are caught, they will be imprisoned or worse. Here it says that during the fighting with Germany, ninety thousand French soldiers were killed and hundreds of thousands of French soldiers were captured and made prisoners of war. It also mentions that the Germans have set up detainment camps in France and that Jews should go into hiding."

Diop took the paper from Claude and shook his head. "So we have signed an armistice with Germany. We have a divided country and we are still in danger. We heard a few weeks ago that our friend, Henri, was among the French soldiers captured."

Claude took the paper and handed it to Josette. "We must remember, there is a world war going on and we are part of it. Its horror will continue to confront us. Every day I wonder, are we going to live or die? Will our children be safe? How long will this war go on? I am hoping that the Americans will come to help liberate France."

The paper shook in Josette's hands. "I am so scared. It says the Jews should hide. We know how Hitler treats the Jews. Because my father was Jewish, I am a target of this German-Vichy terror."

Lourdes felt the impact of the war. Nazi flags were hung next to the Vichy flag and there were more French police and military patrolling the streets. Many in the Free Zone feared the French police more than the German SS or Gestapo because they were native Frenchmen who understood the local dialects fluently. They had extensive knowledge of the towns and countryside, and knew or were friends of the local town people. They also recruited informants throughout Lourdes and Bartrès. There was a military feel to the town, and the people prayed for the safety of their families and themselves.

One gray afternoon in September 1940, a slightly built man in his new blue Vichy police uniform, complete with brown shirt and wide tan beret, entered the bakery. Claude and Josette were both standing next to the checkout counter as the man placed stapled, printed papers on the counter. He glanced around the bakery, and in a stern voice asked if they were the owners. Claude looked at the papers and replied, "Yes, we are the owners. How can we help you?"

The officer moved the papers toward them. "Here are the new regulations issued by the Vichy government that apply to business owners in all the towns and cities within the Free

Zone of southern France, if the businesses are owned by Jews or have Jewish employees. It also applies to gypsies, communists, and homosexuals. The Town Hall registry that you completed indicates that the co-owner of this business is Jewish. Jews are now forbidden to own businesses. These requirements are now law and must be strictly followed and, as you will read, they restrict and limit many of your professional activities and access to certain public places. Also, everyone over the age of sixteen must register and carry a *Carte d'Identité de Français* (French identity card). Your card will indicate that you are a Jew. You have thirty days to comply."

As Josette listened, she trembled, struggling to contain her fear and anger. Defiantly, she addressed the officer. "I am not Jewish; I am a Catholic. So this does not apply to me!" The officer stepped back, opened his military bag, and held up a copy of the Lourdes registry.

"Madame, as you can see for yourself, this registry lists your name as Josette Renée Engel Garmon. It lists you as the co-owner of this bakery along with your husband. Your father was Jewish; therefore, you are Jewish. The regulations clearly spell out the definition of who is a Jew. Catholic is merely your religion. What do you not understand? Your co-ownership dissolves in thirty days. You will have to find employment elsewhere. Understood?" Josette shook her head in disbelief. How could it be possible that the German terror was now the Vichy terror and had come for her family?

Marcel and Nicole were at school when the police officer delivered the notice to their parents. At dinner that evening, Claude and Josette described their encounter to the children. Knowing how difficult it was for Josette, Claude led the conversation. He looked at his beautiful children. "So we know that Germany has won the war with France. We see the German flags hung on many of the buildings. We see Germans riding in their trucks. We know that France is divided into two zones, the North and the South, where we live. We know that the Germans do not like Jewish people and are doing many bad things to them." Marcel listened intently, his mind filled with questions.

"Papa, why don't they like Jewish people? The Lord said to love our enemies." Claude shook his head and responded as best as he could.

"Marcel, I can't give you a good answer. Most of the reason is that Adolf Hitler, the German dictator, hates the Jews. You know about the last Great War. From what I have heard, Hitler believes the Jews caused that war and hurt German businesses by the way they handled the German money they controlled. He also feels that Jews are inferior. They call it Aryanism, and he thinks the Germans are superior to other people."

Marcel was having a difficult time trying to understand what his father was telling him. Nicole, disinterested, was distracted with the salt shaker. Josette interrupted Claude. "Children, listen, and please pay attention to what I am about to tell you." Sensing the seriousness in their mother's voice, the children sat up straight.

"Soon I will not be allowed to work in the bakery, so I can spend more time on my painting and with you. If there are ever German or Vichy soldiers that enter our bakery and you are here in the apartment, Papa will press the button that is under the counter next to the cash register. That will ring the bell we have installed in the apartment kitchen. You both know where it is and have heard it ring. From now on, a ringing bell means trouble and danger. If you hear it, go immediately to hide in the closet off of the balcony until Papa or I come to get you. You must be as quiet as a mouse. If you are downstairs in the bakery, run out the back door and up the steps to the apartment door and then to the closet. I will tape an envelope to the back of the door and place a clock on the shelf. There will be some food and water. Be sure to lock the door. If Papa and I are taken away, hopefully it will not be for long. If we are gone for more than twelve hours, open the envelope and follow the directions that I have written. Do you both understand?" Wide-eyed and solemn, they nodded yes.

Forcing a smile, Josette reached for her children's hands. "Papa and I have a surprise for you! This weekend, we are going to take you to the circus." Nicole jumped up with excitement. Surprised, Marcel asked, "Papa, are you sure there is a circus coming with a war going on?" Claude smiled reassuringly.

"Good question, Marcel. I was surprised as well, but several customers told me about it, and they are going with their children. They reminded me that there was a German circus traveling all over France during the summer—part of Hitler's propaganda to gather French support. It will be just outside of Bartrès, so very close to here."

On Saturday morning the family traveled to the circus grounds. There were long lines, many tents and fences, and German soldiers standing guard at the entrance asking for identity cards and searching for weapons. As they waited to enter, several clowns walked among the crowd, handing out candy bars to the children. There was also a magician making a clown disappear behind a curtain.

The children were so excited. "They haven't been this happy in months," Josette said to Claude. "I am glad we came." They walked over to several circus animals all gathered in a large fenced area. The children moved closer as a giraffe came toward them. Nicole waved her hands. "Come here, Mr. Long Neck! I want to pet you." The giraffe responded to her command and leaned close enough so that she could touch him. Marcel petted a small pony with a braided mane. He saw a tiger and a lion in the distance. As they meandered around the grounds, they stopped to see a magician swallowing a small mouse and then pulling it out of his pocket. The sights and sounds were amazing!

They made their way toward the seating as the show was about to begin. Nazi flags nearly encircled the ring master. Wearing a tuxedo with a Nazi arm band, he directed the crowd's attention to the high wire act. They gazed up at the trapeze performers who dazzled them with their acrobatics. Several young women swung in circles from heavy red silk ropes. The animal parade began with the elephants carrying young girls in colorful outfits on their trunks, followed by bears walking on their hind legs; lions, tigers, and their tamers; and chimpanzees and small dogs dressed in tutus. Marcel and Nicole clapped and cheered. Much too quickly the afternoon passed and the performers waved goodbye. The Garmon family held hands as they headed home and left the circus behind.

Nicole looked up at Josette. "Maman, thank you, and Papa too. This has been the best day ever!" Claude looked at Marcel.

"What was your favorite circus animal?" Marcel squeezed his father's hand. "I liked the lions the best. They are strong and fearless, just like you, Papa." Claude took a deep breath and silently vowed never to forget Marcel's words. He prayed that there would be more days like this ahead.

Six
December, 1941

The Orphanage of St. Stephen

After Claude and Josette took over the operation of the bakery in 1939, they developed loyal customers throughout the town of Lourdes. Many of their church social activities required food and pastries. Through their church connections, they were introduced to religious and business leaders responsible for local schools, boarding schools, hospitals, and orphanages, as well as the many hotels in Lourdes.

Beginning in late winter of 1941, on most Saturday mornings it was Diop's job to deliver bakery goods throughout Lourdes and Tarbes, which is a short drive of twenty kilometers (twelve miles) to the north. Frequently, Marcel would travel with him, and Diop enjoyed his company and help. Occasionally he would encounter a road block or a search of his small delivery truck by the Vichy police, but that was a small irritant. If he were harassed by the police, he would offer them a pastry which he carried in a bag next to him. As the war progressed, however, the trip became more dangerous with French Resistance fighters bombing a bridge or committing other acts of sabotage on Diop's route.

Despite the danger, the deliveries continued at the insistence of their customers. One delivery Diop and Marcel enjoyed was to the Orphanage of St. Stephen, just outside of Tarbes. It was a small campus including boys and girls, each in their own facility separated by beautiful walkways, gardens, and a small chapel that sat next to the convent. Educational classes were provided to the children. It was staffed by nuns, lay persons, and volunteers. Upon arrival, they were usually greeted by the Mother Superior Anne Marie Lobette of the Sisters of Love and Charity, donned in her blue-grey habit and long, beaded rosary that hung from her waist. Mother was small in stature, thin, and wore the white cornette headwear that tightly wrapped her face. It reminded Marcel of a butterfly.

The delivery was always the same, and Mother counted every item before paying Diop. On most days, Mother had a drink to offer them. She always asked Marcel about his sister and parents, and she inquired about Diop's health. Over time, a friendship developed.

On one particular visit, Mother handed Marcel and Diop cups of hot coffee and walked over to her desk. She picked up an envelope and handed it to Marcel. "Marcel, please give this to your father. It is very important, so please be very careful with it." Marcel placed the envelope inside his pants pocket. As soon as they returned to the bakery, Marcel ran in and found Claude pouring dough into a pan. He showed him the envelope. "Papa, Mother Anne at the orphanage told me to give this to you. She told me it is very important." Claude wiped his hands on his apron and opened the envelope. He read: *Once again my angels need wings. Please stop by so we can discuss. Yours in Christ.*

Later that evening Claude and Josette were sipping their tea as the children worked on a puzzle in their bedroom. In a soft voice, Claude told Josette about the envelope Marcel delivered from Mother Superior and handed her the note. "She must have more airmen or Jewish children she wants to trek to the British Consulate in San Sebastian. I will go over for a short visit on Monday. If that is what this is about, that will be the fifth transport she has arranged where I was involved. God knows how many more she has helped and who else assists her. If the Germans uncover her network, a quick death will come to her and to others in her Resistance operation."

Josette shuddered each time Claude talked about transporting downed pilots and children across the Pyrénées Mountains. She took Claude's hand. "Please Claude, I beg of you, tell her this will be the last time you will assist her. Every day we hear about unannounced German visits to suspected members of the French Resistance and their disappearance."

"Josette, please know that our group does not take chances and we protect each other, so please, be calm." She frowned at him. "Remember, I am a Jew, so I must worry! Do you think Diop knows that you are taking these walks with airmen and children? I think you should tell him. He is like family, and he needs to know you are doing this dangerous work."

Claude squeezed Josette's hand. "He knows. I had a long talk with him. As a matter of fact, he expressed interest in joining us. He wants to avenge his father's death." Josette pulled away. "Claude, you hurt my feelings. Why didn't you tell me? Keeping that conversation from me is patronizing. I know you want to protect me, but as your partner, I need to be included in these conversations."

On Monday, Claude arrived at the orphanage and was greeted at the convent door by a young man, tall, thin, with dark hair and long arms. "Monsieur Claude, bonjour! My name is Gabriel. Mother Anne Marie is expecting you. Please follow me." Gabriel led Claude down a long hallway and down a flight of stairs into a small room in the cellar, tucked behind the coal furnace and with a torch light on a table. The orphanage had a maze of rooms and secret hiding places.

Mother stood when Claude entered the room. "Thank you for coming, Claude. Let me make some brief introductions." There were two men seated at the table and Gabriel stood next to them. They stood to shake Claude's hand. Mother Anne Marie pointed to each and spoke in French and then in textbook English. "You have met Gabriel. He is eighteen, French, Jewish, and hiding here. He has relatives living in England. The other two gentlemen are British airmen: Lieutenant Brennan Stewart and Flight Leader Grant Hopkins. Monsieur Stewart was the last to arrive, but the others have been here for several weeks and are anxious to head to Spain. Lieutenant Stewart told me he speaks weak French and I know you, Monsieur Claude, speak poor English!" Mother gave Claude a deliberate stare with a small smile. "Monsieur Claude, do you think you could begin their journey next week?"

Claude looked at the group. "Mother, this will be my fifth trip as a *passeur* (guide), and sorry to say, my last. Gentlemen, we travel at night, and depending on the weather it usually takes four or five nights to get you to the British Consulate at San Sebastiăn, Spain. It is winter and the mountains are snow-packed and very treacherous. I will only be with you for two nights until we reach Saint-Jean-de-Luz. At that stop, another passeur will take over. There are many strong links in our chain. I am just the first. The distance from Tarbes to Saint-Jean-de-Luz is approximately 137 kilometers (85 miles). Our network has safe houses along the way, so most days will be spent sleeping in a safe house, although for a few nights you may be sleeping under the stars. We know where most of the checkpoints and

German or French patrols are, so we have a strong success record. Remember, you will be in extreme danger the moment you leave here. I will return next Monday afternoon, and we will begin the march Monday evening. So be well rested, fully fed, and warmly clothed. Mother has a stockpile of clothing and boots. Hopefully you will be spending Christmas in your home country. *Adieu!*" (Good-bye!)

Claude opened the door and Mother followed him. "Claude, is something troubling you? How is your family? I was surprised to hear that this will be your last trip with my angels!" They made their way to the front entrance.

"Mother, thank you for asking. My family is well, but Lourdes is a changed place with more Vichy police on patrol. Along with the German soldiers, they are making more arrests. As you have heard, German officers are billeting in some of our most beautiful homes. They are sending our food to Germany and to the German soldiers in the Occupied Zone, so there are famine-like conditions here. I know you need food and your children are malnourished. I was told that the Hôtel Beauséjour and the Hôtel Le Riv Droite, which are so close to our bakery, now house approximately 140 political detainees from the American consulates in Vichy and Lyon. There are rumors that they may be moved to the detainment camp in Drancy. Daily, the danger increases. My wife Josette is a Jew by German definition, and the Vichy government has imposed regulations concerning her activities and movement. She can no longer work in the bakery. She is scared and worried. It is becoming more difficult to leave the children and her alone. Now, at Mass on Sunday, we have Vichy police standing at the door and randomly checking our identity cards. One of our dear priests has recently disappeared."

Mother reached for Claude's hand. "Monsieur Claude, I understand the fear, and it grows as the war continues. Thank you for your courage and for helping our angels. I will have them ready for you next Monday. *Au revoir, mon ami!*" (Farewell, my friend!). Claude gave her hand a small kiss and quickly walked to his delivery truck.

Following his mountain trek, on Thursday evening Claude returned to the bakery apartment. He wearily climbed the steps, opened the door, and found Josette sitting at the kitchen table, painting a portrait of a mountain scene. Claude dropped his backpack on the floor, walked over to Josette, and looked at her painting. "Oh, how appropriate. That looks just like the area I left yesterday."

Josette jumped up and put her arms around him. "I wasn't expecting you so early. Did all go well?"

"For the most part it was a smooth trek. We avoided three check points and the trails were snow-covered and icy. The British airmen were up to the challenge, but the Jewish boy fell the first night and hurt his shoulder. I thought he broke something, as he was in much pain. I gave him one of my pills and placed his arm in a sling. That mishap really slowed us down. We reached Saint-Jean-de-Luz about four hours behind schedule. The passeur at the safe house was very concerned. So my part of the transport went well except for the fall, with no issues on my return. How are things here?"

"Thank God you are home safely. The children are fine and I am good. That Vichy police officer stopped by and told Diop that you must now only bake for the town of Lourdes with the hotels being your first priority. I will show you the notice. There are few tourists, so you will provide bread and other bakery items to the American diplomats and the Germans who occupy most of the hotel space. You also have to talk to Diop about the new baker you hired. Diop tells me he has some issues. Did you tell Mother Superior that this was your last trip?"

Claude sat down on the sofa with a buttered bagel in his hand. "Yes, I did tell her and explained the reason. She said she understood. I know she will continue to receive soldiers and Jewish children that need to be hidden and transported. My hope is that her network can give her the help she needs. She told me she now has forty-two children registered at the orphanage and six in hiding. Food is her biggest worry. I told her our situation here is not good, but that I would try to help her if I could. She is such a strong woman and is doing very dangerous work. I admire her and her love for the children."

The next morning Claude and Diop were baking. "Diop, Josette tells me that René Dubois, our new baker, seems to be bothering you. I only worked with him briefly and he seemed fine. I tasted some of his pastries and I thought they were delicious. So what troubles you about him?"

Diop pulled a tray from the oven. "He is unpredictable. Last week when you were not here, he suddenly walked out and was gone for over an hour. He doesn't stay longer in the evening to make up for the lost time and offers no explanation as to his whereabouts. I also noticed his absence on two of the days you were working. You are the owner, so I am just bringing it to your attention. It would be good if I knew when he must leave."

"Thank you for letting me know, Diop. I should have told you sooner, so forgive me. René is a member of the Resistance, but not in my cell. A friend of mine told me about him and said he was a baker looking for work. He is active in Mother Anne Marie's network, and I was aware of that when I hired him. Sometimes he may have to leave quickly and unexpectedly. You may from time to time see someone enter the bakery, ask for René, and hand him a note. The Resistance takes up most of his time, and I look at his work here as part-time and a way for him to earn a few francs."

Diop suspected as much but wanted to hear it from Claude. René, in conversation with Diop, expressed his hatred of the Germans. He told him that his older brother, a French commander, was killed in one of the major battles in the Ardennes forest in 1940. Diop also shared with René the death of his father.

"Let's take a coffee break, Diop. Sorry, but our chicory coffee is all we have." They sat down at the table with the coffees and some pastries. Claude studied Diop's face.

"Recently I told you about my Resistance activities, and now you know about René. Mother Anne Marie needs some occasional assistance. Would you be interested in joining her Resistance group? I know she would welcome you. Before you commit, remember how dangerous this undercover work is. If we are discovered, we could be executed."

Diop sipped his hot coffee. "Claude, I can no longer remain passive and would like to become involved. My German hatred runs deep, but my concern is here. We are busy with the new directive to bake only for the hotels. You know how the Vichy police will strictly enforce this. If I need to miss time here, how will you keep the business running? Josette can no longer help."

Claude moved forward in his chair. "The new directive that we can only bake for the hotels and for the citizens of Lourdes will actually help our business. So in a strange way, that is good news. It should help us purchase the baking supplies we need because of the priority ration cards the police gave me. I will hire a full-time employee as soon as I can find one. With three bakers, we just need some good back-up help. Let me know if you know of anyone."

Diop stood and clutched his empty cup. "Claude, I will send a message to Mother and ask if I can meet with her."

Seven
December, 1941

Diop Joins the Resistance

Christmas passed with little festivity. The Garmon family attended midnight Mass together, along with Diop. Nicole and Josette sang in the choir. As always, a Vichy policeman randomly checked identity cards as they entered the church and another policeman stood on the altar. There was a delicious Christmas dinner, mostly prepared by Diop with some help from Josette and Claude. The gloom of war continued to cast its shadow on Lourdes and all of France.

On the last Friday in December 1941, Diop received word that Mother Anne Marie wanted to see him. Early on a Monday morning, he took the bakery truck and made the drive to the orphanage. Diop knocked on the door and was greeted by a young black boy. With a broad smile, he motioned Diop into the convent, took Diop's hand, and walked him toward Mother's office. The boy was dressed in a black cassock and white surplice. Mother stood and pointed them toward a small room next to her office.

"Diop, thank you for your promptness. I see you have met Raphael. We both just came from Mass in the chapel. As you can see, Raphael was the altar server. Raphael, did you wish greetings to Monsieur Diop?" Raphael was a bit shy as he extended his hand. He saw few black men at the orphanage. Mother gestured toward the chair next to her. Diop took his seat and looked at Raphael.

"Tell me Raphael, how do you like assisting the priest at Mass? I hope you had a good Latin teacher."

"Sister Agatha was my Latin teacher, but I wish I could recite the prayers in French." Diop and Mother laughed.

"Thank you, Raphael," said Mother. "You may change now and go have your breakfast." He waved goodbye as he closed the door.

"Mother, how many children of color do you have here?" Mother placed a small envelope on the table between them. "Raphael is the only one we have at the moment. His story is a sad one. He is almost twelve now, and has been here almost a year. His father was an American soldier who came to France at the end of the Great War and made France his home. He was a talented jazz musician who sang and played the trumpet. He performed in the most popular clubs in Paris. He married a French woman, and Raphael was their only child. Both his parents died in a horrific train accident when a Royal Air Force (RAF) plane bombed the train while on its way from Giverny to Paris. The train was carrying German soldiers, as well as civilians, in a troop carriage. As you can imagine, Raphael is struggling with his loss. Every child who enters this orphanage has a story to tell. His is a story of a young life scarred by unthinkable sorrow."

Touched by Raphael's story, Diop remembered his own pain brought on by the death of his father. He wondered how he could reach out to Raphael. Mother interrupted his thoughts and handed him the envelope. "First, I wish to thank you for offering to help my angels. I have several Jewish children hidden here who are waiting to make the trek to Spain. Lately, more children seem to be coming my way. I just developed a new contact who will provide me with false identity papers for them. Each Jewish child will receive a new Christian identity. If a name sounds Jewish, it is replaced with a French-sounding one. There is a monastery in Urt that has monks who will create the papers I need so the children may begin their journey. It is a quick train ride of two hours from the Tarbes station. This envelope contains your train tickets. Brother Jerome has been sent the information needed to create the birth and baptismal certificates. They are expecting you next Monday. Do you think that is possible?" Diop placed the envelope in his coat pocket. "Yes Mother, I will be there. Is there anything else of importance that I should know?"

Mother leaned forward and almost whispered, "You need to know your code name. The brother will ask you to tell him your confirmation name. You must tell him it is 'Michael.' In my Resistance group, that will be your code name. If you give him any other name he will escort you to the door. You also must remember my code name. It is 'Protéger' (to protect). Also, I know the Germans try to keep news of the war from the French, but we do listen to the BBC world news. I am sure you have heard that the United States has now joined in the conflict after the Japanese bombing of Pearl Harbor on December 7. As the United States mobilizes its military, there may be some positive impact on our efforts to free us from our German occupiers. The British are helping our Resistance movement, and now perhaps the Americans will provide some assistance as well."

Diop returned to the bakery and told Claude about his visit. "Claude, I will only be gone for one day. I will leave early and return late. I know you understand the urgency." Claude touched Diop's shoulder. "Safe travels, my friend!"

The train left Tarbes and arrived at the Urt station by mid-morning. It was an uneventful ride to a beautiful town in the heart of the Basque country—a place that Diop had never visited. He could see from the window the silent giants of the Pyrénées Mountains with peaks that pierced the sky. He walked along the platform and asked the station master for directions to the Abbey of St. Anthony. Crossing the tracks, Diop walked into the town past the Hôtel de Ville and down a slight hill where the crushed stone pathway followed the river Adour toward the Bay of Biscay. He was taken aback with the beauty.

The stone structure of the friary came into view. Diop walked up to the entrance and pulled the rope attached to the bell hanging by the gate. An elderly monk, dressed in a tan tunic tied at his waist and worn sandals on his feet, hobbled toward him. A ragged blanket was wrapped around his shoulders. He slowly opened the gate. "Bonjour and God bless. Brother Jerome is expecting you. Please follow me." They walked up several stone steps to a large, carved wooden door. Diop followed as the monk opened the door and shuffled down the narrow corridor and into a large room with a burning fireplace. On this cold day it was a welcoming sight. There were wooden chairs neatly placed in rows. "Please take a seat. Brother Jerome will be with you shortly."

Diop removed his heavy coat and left it and his paper sack on the chair next to him. He sat as close to the fireplace as possible. A large statue of St. Anthony stood between two stained glass windows, a framed script hanging next to it. Diop walked over to read it.

The Lord manifests Himself to those who pause while in peace and humility of heart. If you want the face of Christ to

*appear in your countenance, pause, collect your thoughts in
silence, and shut the door of the soul to the noise of exterior
things.*

*The greetings of the angels and the blessings of God are not
for those who live in public squares that are outside of themselves,
where they may become agitated and distracted. God, in order to
be able to speak to the soul and fill it with the knowledge of his
love, leads it to solitude, detaching it from the preoccupations of
earthly things. He speaks to the ears of those who are silent and
makes them hear his secrets. ~from the Sermons of St. Anthony*

Diop was told by Mother that the monks at this friary live
in silence and speak only when spoken to, their lives being only
about prayer and work. He also remembered that they make a
delicious cheese from a secret recipe that is known throughout
France for its taste and texture. Engrossed in his musings, Diop
did not see Brother Jerome standing behind him. "Bonjour,
monsieur. I am Brother Jerome. *Votre prénom, si'il vous plait*
(Your first name, please) and your confirmation name."

"I am Diop, and my confirmation name is Michael."

Brother Jerome gave Diop a quick embrace. "Welcome,
Diop, to our abbey. Mother Anne Marie has been in touch with
me. I was expecting you. Do you have her envelope?" Diop lifted
his shirt and removed the envelope taped to his stomach and
handed it to the Brother who immediately opened it and read
the note from Mother. Brother motioned to Diop to follow him.
They walked up a flight of stairs, down a corridor, and into a
crowded room filled with glass test tubes, cylinders, containers
of black ink, lactic acid, stacks of paper, rubber stamps, and a
large magnifying glass.

Brother Jerome opened a file cabinet and produced a large
book which, when opened, contained a hollowed-out center. In

it were several documents which Brother removed and placed in a wooden box with a false bottom. He then secured a hymnal on top of the hidden documents along with loose sheets of music. He placed the box in Diop's paper sack.

Diop was amazed at how quickly this transaction took place. Brother asked Diop if he had any questions. Diop shook his head no. The two left the room and exited at the back of the abbey. They walked down a garden path toward a large gate. Brother opened the gate and pointed to the narrow road that Diop had taken when he arrived. The men shook hands. "Au revoir, and may God be with you."

Diop found his way to the station and waited for the next train to Tarbes. He sat on a wooden bench close to the tracks. On the far end of the platform he saw two uniformed policemen hitting a man with their truncheons. He watched as they carried the poor man away and then heard gun shots. Diop saw another policeman walking toward him. The large man, in a Vichy police uniform, stood next to him. "Let me see your carte d'identité and show me what is in your sack." Diop unbuttoned his coat and found his identity card. He gave it to him with a shaking hand.

"My sack contains my hymnal and some church music. I am a member of a church choir not far from here." Diop lifted the box from the sack and the policeman took it from him. He took the lid off and pulled out the sheet music and the hymnal. Diop prayed that he wouldn't notice the false bottom. The policeman, satisfied, returned everything to Diop and walked away. Diop said a silent prayer of thanksgiving as he saw his train moving toward him.

It was early evening as Diop arrived at the orphanage where the bakery truck was parked. He saw Mother Anne Marie standing on the front steps talking to a young girl. He hurried up to her carrying his sack. She saw him and walked toward him as the girl went into the orphanage. "Diop, you are back much earlier than I expected. How was your journey? Did you encounter any problems? Let's go to my office."

Mother closed the office door and walked over to her desk. Diop reached in the sack and handed her the box. Mother lifted the lid and removed the sheet music and the hymnal. She pried open the false bottom and removed an envelope, carefully opening it and removing several official-looking documents which she placed in neat rows on her desk. There were six rows, one for each hidden child. Diop saw birth and baptismal certificates and some other documents, including one carte d'identité.

"Diop, everything I need for my angels is here. It appears that all went well. I was worried about you. As you know, the trains are dangerous. There are usually Vichy police roaming about and checking identities." Mother smiled and changed the subject. "How is Brother Jerome? Did he give you any cheese? Their cheese is famous. The orphanage just received several boxes from him."

"He appeared to be well, but we really did not converse to any extent. It was all business, so I am not surprised that there was no offer of cheese. I was quite impressed with his chemistry laboratory! The abbey and grounds are beautiful, as well as the town of Urt.

"Concerning my train ride, I did have a scare on my return. I saw the police attacking a man on the platform and heard gun shots. I then had a policeman approach me and ask for my identification. He wanted to see what was in my sack, so I pulled out the box and he looked inside. He seemed satisfied. He returned everything to me and left. I was so frightened, but the Lord was watching over me."

Mother shook her head. "That was a close encounter! Thank God he didn't keep the box and you were not arrested! In many ways, our Resistance is a collection of small dangerous pieces, and when executed properly, all are effective. Thank you for a job well done. Let me ask you a question. Our Resistance cell is in need of some help. It is field work on a large farm near Bartrès. If you are interested, I will have someone deliver a message to you at the bakery."

"Yes, I am interested. Let me know how I can help."

Eight
February, 1942

General De Gaulle
Sends Assistance

Morning blossomed as a nun from the orphanage made a surprise visit to the bakery. Claude was standing behind the display case and moved over to the counter to greet her. She handed him an envelope. "This is from Mother Anne Marie and is for Monsieur Diop." Claude showed her out and went to find Diop, who was washing some bake pans. "A surprise visit from one of the nuns, and she asked me to give this to you."

Diop dried his hands and opened the envelope. He read a hand-written note from Mother: *The farm is in need of your help. Please stop by this Saturday. Let me know if you are not available.* He handed the note to Claude. "With your permission, I will meet with her when I make the Saturday delivery. It shouldn't take long." Claude returned the note. "Diop, take as long as needed."

The following Saturday, Diop loaded the truck and drove to the orphanage. Claude was ignoring the order to only bake for the hotels. He wanted to help Mother Anne Marie, who continued to have difficulty finding enough food and groceries for her children and staff. So, when possible, he sent her a truck full of pastries and other grocery items.

Diop arrived, parked the truck, and walked up to the front door of the convent. He knocked three times and Mother opened the door. "Bonjour. Please come in. I have two strong, young boys who will unload your truck while we talk. Is that acceptable?"

"Mother, that is fine. I appreciate their help. I assume this visit is about the Resistance issue you touched on the last time I was here?"

Mother pulled out two chairs from in front of her desk and handed him a glass of water. "Yes, this Resistance effort is very important. It involves the landing of an airplane and the delivery of much-needed monetary help from our friends in England. There is a large farm near Laruns. You are to arrive there by six in the evening next Sunday. The farmer will be expecting you. There will be a small group of four who will meet in his barn. Once there, the farmer will give you the instructions for the assignment. You should finish before midnight. His name is Monsieur Rossier, and he has your code name. Here is an envelope with directions to his farm from Lourdes. Thank you for helping my angels. God bless!"

Sunday arrived and Diop told Claude about the details. Claude mentioned that he knew the farmer who owned almost two hundred acres there, mostly orchards nestled in the foothills of the Pyrénées. The farmer had a market that sold apples, peaches, and all types of jellies. Claude gave Diop the keys to the truck. "Be safe, my friend!"

Diop was happy to see that the roadway was mostly empty this beautiful evening as the sun was beginning to set behind the hills. He noticed a small sign on the road next to a large walnut tree: Ferme de Rossier (Rossier Farm). Diop turned the truck and drove slowly down a long dirt drive lined with trees. In the distance sat a stately stone home. There was a young woman seated on the porch. She stood, ran down the steps, and motioned him to stop. With a nervous voice, she told him to park behind the house near the barn. He parked the truck, and as he walked into the barn he saw two men standing behind a tractor. Diop noticed a wagon filled with cut firewood attached to the tractor, and that the men were carrying rifles. As he moved closer to them, he recognized René from the bakery.

An elderly man wearing a straw hat, a dirty work suit, and muddy boots walked over to greet him. He extended his hand and spoke in a deep voice, "Votre prénom, si'il vous plait."

Diop stared at the farmer. "My name is Diop." René walked up to them, rifle in hand, and explained to the farmer that he knew Diop and that they worked together at the bakery.

Farmer Rossier gathered the group. "The work this evening is to provide a landing field for a Westland Lysander aircraft flying here from Gibraltar, compliments of the British. The Brits call the plane the "spy-taxi." There will be the pilot and one passenger. I am told that the passenger is one of General de Gaulle's soldiers who will be coordinating Resistance work in this part of France. He is also bringing much-needed cash that will help provide the funds we need to operate. René, after we confirm the amount sent to us, you will take the money immediately to Mother Anne Marie. I will ask Diop to help me square out the landing strip. We will have four fires burning on its corners to pinpoint the target where the airplane will land. These planes are perfect for short-field landings on rough farm fields. We will hear the plane before we see it. It is painted all black with no lights. Just as the pilot is about to touch down, he will turn on his landing lights. We will need to turn the plane around quickly for take-off. This is the third landing I have had here within the last four months. I pray that all goes well this evening."

The farmer drove the tractor out into the field with Diop following behind, almost running to keep up. At each designated spot, they built a fire, returning several times to add more firewood. The fires roared and lit up the dark night.

The farmer smoked his cigarette as he and Diop stood next to the tractor. Diop looked up. "Did you hear that?" The farmer dropped his cigarette. "Yes, I think I see it." The plane flew low over the field and landed in the middle of the four signal fires. The passenger slid back the canopy and made his way down the small ladder. The farmer and Diop ran over and maneuvered the plane into position for take-off. In minutes the plane was back in the air.

The new arrival carried a large backpack and had a pistol in a leather holster. He wore a blue-gray uniform, a beret, and field boots. He shook the farmer's hand with an introduction. "Thank you for the greeting this evening. It appears that all is going according to our plan. General de Gaulle sends his regards. I am Lieutenant Aubert Giraud and will be coordinating your activities with the command in London."

Back at the barn, Aubert extended his hand to Diop. "Monsieur, please tell me your name. I am surprised to find a black man working in the French Resistance."

Diop rolled his shoulders. "My name is Diop, code name 'Michael.' We are few in number, but I do hate the Germans. They killed my father in a bombing attack on Paris some months ago. I am passionate about my commitment to defeat them at any cost."

After moving the tractor into the barn, the farmer handed each man a torch light and walked toward an enclosed area near the back of the barn as the others followed. There were quick introductions, and the Lieutenant reached into his backpack and handed the farmer a large zippered pouch. "A gift from General de Gaulle!"

The farmer counted the money and placed it in neat stacks on a bale of straw. "Thank you, Lieutenant Giraud. I will total the amount here, and all of you can witness. René, tonight you will take this to our Protéger." The farmer placed the money in a large box and handed it to René. He walked over to a bin of corn. "Here, place this corn on top. It will look like a delivery of corn, not money. She will be most grateful."

The soldier acknowledged the thanks and asked, "Can you tell me the plan moving forward? Am I to stay here at your farm? I have been briefed about Mother Anne Marie and am anxious to meet her."

The farmer enlisted Diop's help in pushing an old truck covered in dust forward a few feet from the back wall of the barn and then lifted a trap door in the floor. "Down here I have rifles and ammunition. The aircraft before yours brought this, so it now awaits the arrival of more Resistance forces. Lieutenant, these weapons are now under your control."

The farmer reset the door and they pushed the truck back in place. "You will stay here in our attic for just a few days. Within the next week, you will move to the forest a few miles from here. An encampment there of Resistance fighters is beginning to grow."

As everyone began to leave, the farmer asked Diop to wait. He walked to the back of the barn and returned carrying a pistol. "Diop, you will need this. You are now a member of our new Resistance force, the Organisation de Résistance de l'Armée (ORA). We will keep you busy!"

Nine
July, 1942

The War Comes Closer

Josette grew weary of her self-imposed confinement in the apartment. She was thankful for the company of the children and that she still had her garden with flowers, herbs, and a place to paint. She was concerned that this year of 1942 would bring more restrictions on Jews in the "Unoccupied Zone." She had to report to the *Hôtel de Ville* (City Hall) to be issued a new carte d'identité which had the word "JEW" added in large red type. She continued to read the Resistance papers that occasionally arrived and knew that Jews in the north were suffering. Last year she heard from friends in Paris that German forces confiscated all radios belonging to Jews, followed by their telephones and bicycles. They were forbidden to leave their homes between 8 p. m. and 5 a. m. All shops, parks, theatres, cinemas, and concert halls were closed to Jews.

Late one afternoon in mid-June, Diop approached Josette painting in the gazebo and asked her if she heard that the German military commander in Paris had ordered all Jews over six years of age to wear, on the left side of the chest, a yellow star with the inscription "Juif" (Jew).

"No, I have not heard that. Will the Vichy authorities impose that here? When will this German terror end?"

Josette and Claude continued to hear from customers and friends at church that there were more refugees in Lourdes fleeing from the north and also from the coastal areas of Nice and Marseille. They also were told about the atrocities in Poland, Germany, and the death camps. A name they heard was Auschwitz which, they were told, represented the epitome of all horror.

The summer of 1942 had a strange, almost prison-like feel, as the Vichy police were noticeably more aggressive. They stopped people for no reason and questioned them. If someone did not carry an identity card, there was an immediate arrest. It was not uncommon to see the police beating men and women on the streets. The queues at the various stores lasted for hours, as so many groceries and sundries were in short supply. The bakery no longer received priority rationing and was now only open three days a week. Marcel and Nicole could no longer go to parks and playgrounds alone due to police harassment, and they heard that their school might not reopen after summer holiday.

Several customers brought word to Claude that on July 17 and 18 the Nazis conducted a roundup of Jewish men, women, and children in Paris. He was told that over eight thousand Jews were held in a large stadium, the Vel' d'Hiv' (Winter Stadium) in Paris, with little food and water. They were then transferred to rail cars, their destination unknown. They also heard that Nazi SS troops took control of Nice and conducted raids on Jews who live there.

Late one evening, after kissing the children goodnight, Claude and Josette sat on the balcony overlooking the garden. The sun was setting, the sky radiant with deep blue and purple clouds. They sipped their wine and talked about all of the changes they had witnessed since the Germans entered France and the emotional toll it had taken, especially on Josette and the children.

Claude took a deep breath. "Josette, we must talk about the future. I cannot imagine the horror we have yet to see. I have been thinking that maybe we should create an escape plan. I heard from one of the customers that he will walk away from his home here and move closer to Spain and wait out the war. Someone else told me that his family will move to Marseilles and take a freighter to Greece. Perhaps we should consider something similar?"

Josette shook her head. "No, I do not want to leave here. This is home. Lourdes will once again find its majesty and will never lose its beauty. The life of a refugee is not appealing. This war can't last forever, and someday, hopefully soon, we will regain the lives we enjoyed.

"But I am concerned about the children. Have you noticed that they are more quiet and withdrawn? Marcel sleeps most of the time and is quick to anger. Nicole is always crying and upset. They are bored and afraid to go out. No sports, no bicycles or friends to play with. It is another world for them. And I am very worried about the bakery. Do you think our business will survive?"

"Josette, only God knows if any of us will survive. The bakery is resilient. Pierre and Lucinda had many highs and lows when they owned it. They survived the Great War and the economic downturn in 1929. We must think positively and pray that we will retain our business."

As the year progressed, the economic situation did not improve and the children did not return to school. Claude and Josette stayed informed concerning the progress of the war. Rumors spread that the Allies might invade southern France.

Several of their friends had hidden radios and still connected to the BBC. At 9:15 every night, the BBC broadcasted messages concerning the war throughout France. They hoped to hear news about Allied successes and German failures. The broadcast began with the tones of the first four notes of Beethoven's Fifth Symphony which, to those who knew Morse code, was the sound of "V" for victory: three short clicks and one long. A cryptic message usually followed directed to Resistance groups. Friends and customers always brought Claude the latest news.

Late one morning, Claude hurried up the stairs to the apartment. Josette was fixing the children lunch. He motioned for her to follow him into the bedroom. "I heard some very worrisome news. Did you know that the Germans and the Vichy police have a detention camp in Gurs, just sixty miles from here? A large garrison of soldiers is stationed there. We heard that they are rounding up foreign-born Jews and sending them to Gurs." Josette began to tremble. "This war is closing in on us. I am so afraid!" Claude pulled her close and held her in a warm embrace.

One autumn Sunday after Mass, Diop took Marcel to the field behind the bakery to kick the soccer ball. They fashioned a make-shift goal and Diop had Marcel practice his goal-kicking. As a storm began to roll in, they rushed back to the bakery. Diop complimented Marcel in front of Claude. "Your son will someday lead the French soccer team to the Olympics!" Marcel blushed as Claude gave him a hug before sending him upstairs to the apartment.

"Diop, Josette and I have been meaning to talk to you about the children. We know that this part of France is becoming increasingly dangerous. Each day brings new trauma. We wanted to ask you to watch over the children if something should happen to us—to take them to Mother Anne Marie, where they will be safe. My hope and prayer is that it will never come to this, but we must be prepared."

"Claude, you and Josette have brought me into your family, and for that I will be eternally grateful. I love Marcel and Nicole. Please know that I will care for them if the situation you describe should befall us."

Ten
November, 1942

Josette's Jewish Identity

The winds of war grew more savage and frightful. On Wednesday, November 11, 1942, Diop rushed into the bakery, shaking and barely able to speak. "Claude, everyone at the hotel was talking about the news. The Germans are now occupying all of France. Our 'Free Unoccupied Zone' controlled by the Vichy government no longer exists. German troops have arrived from Bordeaux, and now we have Nazi officers in command here with German soldiers throughout all of southern France. Also, we heard that Italian forces have taken control of Toulon and all of Provence up to the river Rhone. I just saw three black Mercedes limousines pull in front of the Hôtel Albon. The Nazis Wehrmacht and some Gestapo will be the only ones living there! There will be a German garrison of tents just along the river for their troops."

Claude stepped back. "I can't believe what I am hearing. That explains the German lorries loaded with soldiers moving past the bakery this morning. This is not good. I need to tell Josette and the children this awful news!"

Claude found Josette and the children in the garden gazebo. Josette was watching them sketch pictures of flowers and trees. Claude sat on the bench next to them. "Let me see your drawings." The children held them up proudly. "Very well done! Maman is a good art teacher." Claude paused.

"I have something very important to share with you." Marcel put down his sketch pad. "Papa, is something wrong?"

"Yes, more bad news about the war. I want to tell you some important news that I just heard from Diop. The war is now at our doorstep. The Vichy police who have been here since France surrendered have moved on. The German soldiers now occupy all of France. That brings more concern and possible increased danger to Lourdes and to us as a family. I don't want to upset you, but I want to be honest with you. I know this may be difficult for you to understand." Josette shook her head.

"The children have heard enough. Children, please go to your room and I will come up in a minute to fix you something to eat." Marcel and Nicole exchanged looks and obeyed their mother.

Claude glared at Josette. "They need to hear the truth about what is happening. They need to be aware of the new and more serious situation here. Pretending that everything remains the same means we are living a lie. I think we need to revisit our conversation about leaving Lourdes. As of today, our lives became much more complicated and dangerous." Josette frowned at Claude.

"You know how emotional the children are and now you only create more anxiety and fear for them. How much more can they endure? No more discussion about leaving Lourdes!"

As more German troops arrived in Lourdes and the surrounding area, Lourdes began to look more like Berlin. Someone placed a Nazi swastika on the front of the bakery, and the red and black Nazi flags hung from the town hall and along the river walk. Food became scarce as the Nazi troops had first priority. They crowded the restaurants, and young women were afraid to walk the streets. German officers billeted in the hotels and homes.

In early December, Claude opened the front door of the bakery to discover a note taped to the door.

All residents of Lourdes must attend a
mandatory meeting on the plaza
at the Hôtel de Ville this coming Saturday at 10:00 a. m.

The damp, cool Saturday arrived and the Garmons, along with Diop and the children, made the short walk to the Town Hall. The shops were all closed as the people of Lourdes gathered in the center of town. Swastikas and victory propaganda signs hung from balconies. German soldiers, rifles in hand, were standing in front of the majestic brick and stone building with its conical turrets. Nazi flags hung from the windows. Papers were being distributed by women dressed in German uniforms. A Wehrmacht officer, in his dress uniform with its silver braided belt and medals, climbed the steps and stood on the front balcony. He held up the paper that was being handed out. The large crowd stood shoulder to shoulder as friends and neighbors greeted each other with concern and trepidation. The officer made the Nazi salute and began to speak in a booming voice.

"As you know, Germany now occupies and controls all of France. If you follow our directives contained within the paper given to you, your lives should continue as they were. The curfew will continue. Within the next five days, all citizens over the age of sixteen must re-register here at the Hôtel de Ville. At the time of registration, ration cards will be assigned. Following registration, you will be given a new identity card which must be carried with you at all times. As previously required, all weapons of any type, including ammunition, must be turned in. Our soldiers will make random inspections to insure compliance. All crimes and acts of resistance will result in death. *Sieg Heil!* (Hail Victory) Dismissed!"

The crowd murmured and slowly disbursed. Marcel and Nicole walked ahead in silence as their family returned to the bakery. "So now we hear that German justice will be delivered quickly by a German rifle," Josette said bitterly.

"I am not surprised," said Diop. "We have heard that in all the German-occupied territories, public executions on streets and town squares are commonplace, and it applies to men, women and children."

"I am so saddened that the children had to experience this. Another horrible day for them." Nicole suddenly stopped and waited for her mother. "Maman, I am scared!" Josette knelt next to her. "Nicole, I don't want you to be frightened. Our family is strong. Please remember that Lourdes is protected, not by soldiers but by our Father in heaven and His Blessed Mother. They are watching over all of us."

Early Monday morning, Claude and Josette returned to Town Hall. There was a long queue and the line moved slowly. Once inside, they made their way down a long hallway toward a lobby filled with German officers seated at long tables. They sat in wooden chairs next to each other and completed a new questionnaire and registration form. The officer wanted to see Josette's identity card. Claude was dismissed.

"I see that your father is Jewish and your mother is French. Is that correct?" Josette nodded. "So according to German law and regulation, you are Jewish. Are your parents deceased?"

Josette slid her chair closer and spoke clearly. "Oui, both of my parents have passed. Do your records indicate that my religion is Catholic?" The officer responded with a glare.

"Madame, we are not interested in your religion. We are interested in your ethnicity and very interested in your Jewish ancestry. Nuremberg Law defines you as a Mischling. Your ethnicity is mixed—Jew and Aryan. Because you are a Jew, you will be closely watched and your comings and goings will be restricted. Is that understood? Here is your thirty-day ration card. Also, you must display this Star of David on the front door of your residence and business." He handed her a yellow star emblazoned with the word *Juif.* "You are dismissed."

Claude was waiting for her near the front entrance. The look on her face as she walked toward him told him that she was upset. He touched her hand. "How did it go?"

Josette's voice was emotional. "He was most interested in the fact that my father was Jewish and reminded me that under German law that makes me Jewish. Claude, we know how the Germans are treating the Jews! They want to kill all the Jews in Europe. Maybe we should talk about a new place to live. I am so scared at this moment. Look! Even my ration card is stamped *Juif.* He handed me a Star of David that we must place on our front door. Claude, we need to have a very serious discussion with the children and try to explain, as best we can, what the star means."

The next day, Claude tacked the yellow star next to the front door. He noticed that a few other shops had the star displayed as well. It provoked conversation from his customers, and he was told by several loyal patrons that there was a registration list posted in Town Hall. It contained a long list of residents with various designations such as Communist, Freemason, Homosexual, Catholic, and Jew. Josette's name was listed as a Jew. Claude decided to keep this information to himself, feeling that, at this moment, Josette had enough to deal with.

Claude and Josette decided that in spite of all of the changes in their lives resulting from the German occupation on

November 11, they were determined to make the Christmas of 1942 a happy and memorable time for Marcel and Nicole. In the apartment, a small pine tree was erected outside the kitchen, bedecked with red ribbons and tiny candles. Displayed on the kitchen counter was the Advent wreath with its four candles.

Following midnight Mass and a quick sleep, the children rose early and were anxious to see what gifts were left by *Père Noël* (Father Christmas). Marcel no longer believed in the Christmas myth, but Nicole still held on to most of the legends. On Christmas Eve they left their shoes near the apartment door filled with carrots for Père Noël's donkey, Gui. Nicole was delighted to find the carrots gone and their shoes filled with brightly-wrapped chocolate. She squealed with joy, "Père Noël was here!" She also found a large stuffed bear and some new clothes spread out on the sofa. Claude walked in carrying a large box and handed it to Marcel, who placed it on the floor and tore it open. "Oh Papa, it is the telescope that I have been talking about! This is the best gift ever! Thank Père Noël for me."

In early afternoon Diop knocked on the door and carried in two bottles of Bordeaux Blanc. Josette was putting the finishing touches on the main course, rabbit terrine in ginger sauce. Claude handed Diop an apron, and together they prepared the ingredients for the Yule Log cake.

Soon the apartment was fragrant with the aromas of Christmas. Josette lit all of the candles as they gathered for this memorable feast. They joined hands and bowed their heads as Claude prayed, "Lord, please bless this meal and the family gathered here. We thank you for these gifts, and please continue to watch over and protect us."

"Amen," they all said in unison.

Eleven
February, 1943

The Bakery Closes

The year 1943 brought additional stress and worry as the war turned more toward southern France. Claude and Josette worried about friends in Avignon. They heard that Allied aircraft bombed Avignon, Marseille, Amiens, and Eauplet, and over three thousand French civilians were killed. Josette and Claude prayed that the bombings would not come to Lourdes.

Close to home, Marcel and Nicole's school reopened, but teachers were hard to find. The classes, now co-ed, were large in number. Marcel's class had both seventh and eighth graders with one teacher and sixty children. In mid-February, the principal, Sister Regis, sent a letter home to parents which stated that St. Elizabeth's school may have to close again. Several of the teachers were male, and the German authorities issued an order on February 16 that the *Service du Travail Obligatoire* (STO: Compulsory Work Service) had been decreed and required all able-bodied French men between the ages of sixteen and sixty-five be drafted to work in Germany. Claude and Josette knew that this would apply to Diop and René, as well as Claude and so many other men in France.

Claude asked Diop and René to meet with Josette and him one evening in late February as soon as the bakery closed for the day. Josette poured the chicory coffee as they gathered around the table next to the display case. Claude grimly sipped his coffee. "As we know, there is a strong possibility that soon the three of us will be drafted by the Nazis to work in Germany. The bakery no longer has an exemption, and more of the hotels have closed. You can see how our business has suffered. I am told that when we receive the draft notice, we only have fourteen days in which to report to the Wehrmacht camp. Josette and I have decided to close the bakery." Josette, at first quiet, began to cry as she listened.

René poured more coffee into his cup and lit a cigarette. He looked at Claude and Josette with his sad, sea-blue eyes. "Diop and I had a strong feeling that this news was coming, and we have talked about our next steps. Let's hope that the closing will be short-lived and you will be reopening this time next year.

"We told you about meeting Lieutenant Aubert Giraud when he landed on Monsieur Rossier's farm with the cash for Mother Anne Marie. We have been informed that he has now mobilized a strong Resistance force. The Maquis is now part of his United Resistance Movement and received their assets from General de Gaulle. His main force is scattered in the forest just outside of Laruns, just thirty miles from here. He was joined by General Charles Delestraint who will now take command. Diop and I have decided that we will join his Secret Army."

Josette went up to the apartment and returned with a ragged piece of poster paper. "When I was walking to the butcher shop with my ration card, I saw this pamphlet taped to the door of a closed salon." She held it tight with both hands and read it aloud:

"Men who come to the Maquis to fight live badly, in precarious fashion, with food hard to find. They will sleep under trees, in caves, and under the moon and stars. They will be absolutely cut off from their families for the duration of the battle; the enemy does not apply the rules of war to them, and they will be executed upon capture. They cannot be assured any pay; every effort will be made to help their families, but it is impossible to give any guarantee. All correspondence is forbidden. We fight in the shadows for the liberation of France.

Please join us. If possible, bring two shirts, two pairs of underpants, two pairs of woolen socks, a light sweater, a scarf, a heavy sweater, a woolen blanket, an extra pair of shoes, shoelaces, needles, thread, buttons, safety pins, soap, a canteen, a knife and fork, a torch, a compass, a weapon if possible, and also a sleeping bag, if possible. Wear a warm suit, a beret, a raincoat, a good pair of hobnailed boots. Liberty is sacred and we must fight for it. We need YOU!"

She handed the paper to Diop. "This has been posted in many places, and I have seen it before. It sounds like someone is going on holiday rather than joining the Resistance army. I don't think they want you to bring a suitcase full of clothes and camping gear."

René and Claude laughed and René took a deep drag on his cigarette. "Diop and I both know the risks and it will be dangerous, but our country needs to be free of this German occupation and we want to help. The German labor camps are not inviting! When you close the bakery, we will pack and head to Laruns. I have notified Mother of our intentions, and she has met with both Lieutenant Giraud and General Delestraint. She has given me a map leading to his base camp."

Claude took a deep breath. "Josette and I respect your decision, but we will miss you. I know the children will find this hard to understand, and you know they will miss you, too. You both know that not much is going on here. Flour, eggs, and milk are impossible to buy. For now, we are finished with this bakery and it breaks our hearts. You are free to leave whenever you are ready. I know, God willing, our paths will cross again and after the war, when we reopen, we will celebrate your return." The four stood together in a farewell embrace.

On the last day of February 1943, at daybreak, Diop and René loaded their belongings into the bakery truck. Josette, Marcel, and Nicole gave their friends goodbye hugs and waved as the truck pulled away, headed for the Gave de Pau River. As Claude drove them to a drop-off point at the foothills of the Pyrénées near Laruns, René looked out the window and thought how much he would miss the beauty of Lourdes. Diop was quiet as they passed German lorries parked along the river bank. He realized that a war was going on and now he would be a small part of it.

As they got closer to their destination, vast mountains and forest surrounded them. The weather was extremely cold and the mountains were snow-covered and beautiful. Diop and René were overly dressed in as much wool as possible. Their rucksacks were full, and they tried to follow the directions of the Resistance flyer that Josette read to them. Weapons were the only exception, although they each carried hunting knives. René followed his compass, and some three miles from Laruns he told Claude to take a small dirt road that branched off the main highway. The truck bounced along through the scrubland.

"Stop, Claude. This is the spot." They saw a small clearing that led into the forest. Diop and René placed their rucksacks on their shoulders and Claude gave them each a handful of francs. "Not sure where you will spend this," he said with a wry grin. "I will really miss you. Today your lives turn in a different direction. Be safe and watch over each other. May our Lady of Lourdes keep you safe."

They exchanged handshakes and hugs. Claude watched them disappear into the wilderness and walked back to the truck, wondering what their futures would hold.

Twelve
March, 1943

The Resistance Army

Diop and René followed the narrow, muddy path into the forest. As they continued their trek, they reached a swift-flowing mountain stream. They found a spot to cross and jumped over the slippery rocks scattered from each side. As they climbed the river bank the trail started to disappear. They looked at the crude map provided by Mother Anne Marie and guessed that they should keep walking southwest. For over an hour they continued deep into the forest. Clouds gathered quickly and a light snow began to fall. In a clearing they were able see the open rocky summit and decided to take a brief rest. They sat on a large rock and sipped the water from their canteens.

Suddenly Diop jumped up and looked around. "I just heard something. Maybe a deer running nearby." As René stood, he saw two figures moving from behind a large pine tree not more than twenty yards away. The figures walked toward them with their rifles in hand. The two were very young, perhaps in their late teens, slim in ragged blue trousers, drab gray shirts and dark blue Basque berets. One had a hand grenade hanging from his belt. René and Diop walked toward them. Diop whispered to René, "I think we found their camp."

The shorter youth, his rifle pointed at Diop's chest, asked, "What brings you here and why are you walking in the forest?"

Diop responded with a nervous voice. "Our Protéger told us you may need some help to fight the Germans."

The two peppered Diop and René with additional questions: "From where did you travel? Do you have identification? Do you have weapons? Are you prepared to die for France?" Satisfied with the answers, the young men slung their rifles over their shoulders.

"Welcome to our Resistance Army. Follow us." They walked for another forty minutes over snow-covered brush, downed trees, and small streams. Diop and René smelled the smoke from the camp and heard the murmur of voices. In front of them was a clearing with men standing around a camp fire. Four boys encircled the camp with rifles at the ready. Tents and some crudely-constructed tables holding pots and pans were scattered about. One of the soldiers was gutting a rabbit hanging from a tree limb. Large pots of water were boiling over a fire pit. On a sheet someone had painted the Cross of Lorraine, the symbol of the Resistance.

As they moved closer to the fire pit, an older soldier wearing a brown military helmet and a wrinkled dirty gray uniform walked briskly toward them. He stood next to the two Maquis fighters and pointed at Diop and René. "Where did you find them?"

One Maquis stepped forward. "Colonel, we found them about three miles from here, wandering through the forest. They are here to join our group." The colonel asked Diop and René to sit on two primitive log seats, close to the fire and under a tarped roof that provided some protection from the falling snow. He instructed those in the camp to gather around.

With a gruff voice he introduced himself to René and Diop. "I am Colonel Emile Dumond, and I command this camp. I report to General Delestraint who answers to General de Gaulle. Our group at this camp is small in size, now almost thirty, scattered here and around the immediate area. Will each of you stand and tell us who you are and why you are here."

Diop stood first and told them about his family's immigration to France from Cameroon, the death of his father during the German bombing of Paris, and his work at the hotels and bakery in Lourdes. He told them about his covert work with Mother Anne Marie and her cell. He also mentioned his love of soccer and rugby.

In a strong voice, René spoke about his work at the bakery, his Resistance work with Mother, his love of France, and his hate for the Nazi terror. He pointed to the painted sign hanging from a tree. "The wording on that sign describes my passion: *To Live Defeated is to Die Every Day.*"

The colonel dismissed the rest of the group and asked Diop and René to follow him. There were some old wooden folding chairs sitting next to a table. He sat at the head and pointed to the two seats next to him. He removed his helmet and placed it on the table. "Let me give you both a quick look at what we are all about. I mentioned that we have about thirty here in three squads. The average age is twenty-six, and most are here because they don't want the Nazis to send them to Germany. None has a military background except five Spaniards who recently joined us and speak broken French. They fled Spanish reprisals for being on the wrong side of their civil war. They are explosive and demolition experts and know how to launch grenades. I will assign both of you to their squad.

"Our campfires are extinguished by 7:30 each evening because German spotter planes fly over to locate campfires and note compass locations. We also move our camp every two weeks just to drive the German devils crazy. Our mission now is sabotage. We have bombed several of the rail lines that the Germans use for military transport. Our next target is the airfield the Germans have built at Pau. The Luftwaffe uses it for pilot training. It is a grass surface with no paved runways. There is an ammunition dump off of the south landing strip. That is our target. We want to ignite that ammunition and set off a fire they will see all the way to Paris. It will be dangerous, but with the right planning we can make it happen. Enough for now. Let me find a tent for you."

The weeks moved quickly. René and Diop were now part of a squad, the *Défenseur* (Defender): three other Maquis from nearby towns—Emile, Paul, and Georges; and five Spaniards—Paco, Luis, José, Sergio, and Juan. Sergio, who had the most military experience and spoke the best French, led the squad.

To conduct surveillance and set their plan, the Défenseur trekked the twenty miles several times, mainly at night, to the location of the Pau airfield. They would sleep for a few hours in the forest, then head back to the camp, clocking forty miles in less than twenty-four hours. Early one morning, they monitored German troop movement and photographed the target area.

Having returned to the camp, they briefed Colonel Dumond. The Spaniards recommended that a grenade attack would provide the outcome the colonel was looking for. The colonel and Sergio decided that this attack would be carried out by only five members of the squad: Sergio, Paco, José, Diop, and René.

The plan involved their moving at night through the forest from their camp in the foothills of the Pyrénées Mountains to the Pau airfield. Each would carry a torch in his field pack along with ammunition, compass, and a cyanide suicide pill to avoid

German torture if captured. The position of the moon would determine the date, as the night had to be totally dark.

Diop, René, and Paco would provide cover with their rifles and pistols while Sergio and José fired their shoulder grenade launchers using the large caliber projectiles. Forest cover stopped approximately fifty yards from the barbed wire fence that surrounded the airfield and the ammunition warehouse. Their reconnaissance showed them that two German soldiers were always guarding the ammunition storage facility.

On a rainy Wednesday, March 31, 1943, the squad received word from the colonel to commence the attack. The five spent the next eight hours walking toward Pau through the dense forest and arrived close to midnight at the designated spot on the south side of the landing strip. They settled under a tree canopy where they could see the lights of the airfield. Sergio huddled with the others and reviewed the plan one more time. All were dressed in dark camouflage uniforms and helmets.

Their binoculars searched the target area, and to their surprise they saw only one guard napping in a *Kubelwagen* (Jeep) parked next to the warehouse door. They crawled toward the fence, and from ten yards distance Sergio and José launched the grenades at the warehouse while Paco, René, and Diop provided rifle fire cover. As soon as all of the grenades were launched, they made a dash to the meeting point about a half-mile into the forest.

They crawled single file through the darkness and towards the fence. At Sergio's signal, they moved into a line, each ten feet apart. Sergio looked at the guard who was awake and on his radio. The guard saw Sergio and José stand to launch their grenades. Diop, René, and Paco opened fire on the guard crouched behind his Kubelwagen.

The roof of the facility instantly burst into flame and, just as fast, a platoon of nine Wehrmacht soldiers appeared and began firing in their direction as the five fled for forest cover. Sergio was ahead of the group and heard and felt a tremendous explosion. The night sky was bright in the fire storm as bullets were fired at the Resistance fighters.

The night disappeared into lights, sirens, rifle fire, screams, and explosions. As the five ran, Paco screamed, "René has been hit!" Diop turned and saw René lying motionless. Sergio yelled, "Keep moving! We cannot help him!" Bullets struck Sergio as he ran. Diop hit the ground and crawled over to him. He saw blood pooling on the frozen turf and knew he could not help. José and Paco screamed at Diop to leave him. *"Correr por tu vida!"* (Run for your life!). Diop felt the heat of a bullet that entered his shoulder as he ran into the forest.

Thirteen
April, 1943

Nazi Terror at the Bakery

On Monday, April 19, 1943, the bakery had a large "Closed" sign stapled on the locked entrance door. Claude was up early and working to pack and clean the bakery as Josette prepared breakfast and readied the children for school. She would always take their school clothes from the large wooden armoire and place them on the bed. "Nicole!" she called. "Today is your Easter concert so you don't have to wear your uniform. I think you should wear this cute little pink dress with these pretty black shoes." Marcel was already at the breakfast table dressed in his school uniform—a white shirt and blue pants. He heard some commotion down in the bakery. "Maman, did you hear that? It sounds like someone is beating on the door."

Claude was in the back of the bakery and heard what sounded like someone beating on the entrance door with a club. He came out front and saw three German soldiers banging on the door with their rifle butts and a German truck sitting at the curb. He ran to the counter and found the button that rang the bell in the apartment.

Josette and Marcel heard the bell. "Marcel, get your sister. Quiet, now! Into the balcony closet. There must be Germans downstairs with Papa. Remember our plan." Josette gave them each a quick, reassuring hug. "Lock the door, and hide behind the shelves. I am going downstairs to check on your father. Remember—quiet as mice!" She managed a smile. *"Je vous aime"* (I love you).

Josette hurried down the steps and into the bakery. Claude stood behind the counter, arguing with the soldiers. He turned to see Josette standing behind him.

"What is the problem?" she asked. An older officer stepped forward. "I am Lieutenant Higer. We have orders to take a Jew, named Josette Garmon, to our station for questioning. I presume that you are that person." Claude moved from behind the counter and stood in front of Josette. Josette talked over Claude's shoulder. "Yes, I am Josette Garmon, but this is not a good time for me to talk to you. Can I set up an appointment to meet with someone at a later time?"

The soldiers laughed. "Madame, as I said, our commanders have issued an order for your questioning. You must come with us now. You will not be alone. We have several others in our truck who will be joining you. You have no choice in this matter. Please follow us or we will be forced to arrest you."

Claude's face was red with anger. "You heard my wife. This is not a good time. She will not be joining you. I must ask you to leave!"

Two of the soldiers shoved Claude aside and took Josette by the arms. Claude lunged toward the soldiers, pushed one to the floor, and gave him a hard kick. The lieutenant pointed his rifle at Claude's chest and fired. Claude staggered and fell to the floor, blood streaming through his white shirt, his eyes lifeless and staring.

"No, no, no, no!" Josette moaned, trying to go to her husband. The soldiers grabbed her around the arms and legs and carried her to the truck. Josette flailed and cried, "Please! My children! My children! You killed my husband!"

The soldiers pushed Josette into the back of the truck and onto the floor, slamming the door behind her. Four other people already in the truck helped Josette up to a bench and tried to comfort her, but she kept repeating, "They killed my husband. They killed Claude." One of the women, Marta, recognized Josette and whispered to the others, "She owns the Bon Temps Boulangerie, and I know both her and her husband. Why did these monsters have to kill him?"

The truck accelerated into the morning traffic and within a few minutes pulled around to the back of a detainment center the Germans hastily built behind Town Hall. Several soldiers met the truck and led Josette and her companions into the building. They separated the men from the women. Josette and the other two women were pushed into a small holding cell. Lieutenant Higer ordered them to sit until they were called, then shut and locked the door. Josette cried softly into her hands.

Marta sat next to Josette. "I am so sorry, Josette. I cannot believe they would murder Claude." Josette could not stop the tears and could hardly speak. "It all happened so quickly. He was trying to protect me. I must return for him and for my children."

The door opened and Lieutenant Higer walked over to Josette. "Come with me!" She followed him down the hallway to a small office. A uniformed officer was sitting behind a small desk with Hitler's picture hanging on the wall and a Nazi flag next to it. The lieutenant placed a chair in front of the desk and motioned to Josette to sit. She remained standing.

The man behind the desk spoke. "I am Colonel Kimmich. Lieutenant Higer informs me that your husband assaulted one of our soldiers and that you were resisting arrest; therefore, he was justified to use lethal force. Your husband's body will be taken to St. Jean Luc Hospital. One of our German doctors will perform an autopsy."

Overcome, Josette collapsed to the floor. Higer picked her up and sat her on the chair as Kimmich handed her a glass of water. "Please, settle yourself. I must ask you a few brief questions that only require a yes or no answer."

Kimmich pulled a cigarette from a gold case, lit it, and took a deep drag. "According to my records, you are registered as a Jew and your religion is Catholic. You are the mother of two children, a boy and a girl. You were the co-owner of a bakery and live in an apartment at the same location. Is this information correct?"

Josette sipped her water with a shaky hand and found her voice. "Yes, that is correct. Are you charging me with a crime or did you arrest me because I am a Jew?"

Kimmich placed his cigarette in the ashtray and stared at Josette. "Madame, I ask the questions. I am sure you are aware of several Resistance movements that are very active in this part of France. I believe you refer to them as the Maquis. They have escorted Allied soldiers to Spain, blown up our troop trains, and just attacked our air base at Pau. We have received information that you and your husband, as well as your employees, may be involved. Is it your understanding that Diop Medar and René Dubois are members of the Maquis?"

Josette's mind was moving in many different directions. *Should I lie or tell him the truth? Are Diop and René alive? Will they torture me? Will they find and arrest the children?* She looked directly at the colonel.

"I can only tell you that neither my husband nor myself is involved with the Maquis. The only thing I can tell you about Diop and René is that they worked for us until we closed the bakery. I am not aware that they were involved in any Resistance activities and I have not seen them since we closed."

Higer stood over Josette, raised his fist, and struck the side of her face. She fell off the chair, her mouth bloodied. Without flinching, Kimmich growled, "You are a liar. Get this Jewish slut out of here." Higer pulled Josette roughly from the floor, pushed her toward the door, and dragged her back to the cell.

In pain from her swollen jaw and cut lip, Josette asked daily for aspirin from the female guard but was ignored. She and her cellmates, Marta and Agnes, were clothed in drab gray prison uniforms and cloth sandals with wooden soles. Each day began at 6 a.m. They were marched to the refectory where they were fed a putrid meal of cold oatmeal and a small sausage. At 4 p.m. each day, they were fed stale bread and one small piece of chicken breast, but all three barely ate. They sat in the cell from morning to night, taking turns emptying the waste pail, rarely speaking. Josette prayed for the safety of her children, assuring herself that they were being cared for by Pierre and Lucinda. She longed to see them, touch them, hold them, and tell them how much she loved them.

When the women did speak, they talked about their families, the war, and what was to happen next. They kept track of the days, and on Easter Sunday they were particularly quiet, quiet in their disbelief that they were spending this holy day locked in a prison in Lourdes without their families and friends around them. Josette was told that because she was a Jew and helping the Resistance, she would be transported to the prison at Drancy near Paris the next day.

Marta, young and a bit reckless, was supposed to be released within a fortnight. Her "crime", according to the authorities, would be dismissed. She was stopped by a Wehrmacht soldier and did not have her identity card. She argued with him and was arrested.

Agnes was told that she would be sent to the internment camp in Gurs, approximately sixty miles from Lourdes. A neighbor suspected her Resistance involvement and told the Germans. She had been working with a small group in Pau, mainly cooking and washing for Resistance fighters who sometimes stayed at her home. She also distributed their newsletters. She was married with no children. Her husband, a French army officer, was a prisoner of war, held somewhere in Germany.

Josette gave Pierre and Lucinda's address to Marta, with the promise that Marta would stop there as soon as she was released. Josette wanted to give her a letter to take to the children, but she did not want to place Marta in danger. They knew that letters were *verboten* (forbidden).

"Marta, when you see my children, please tell them that I am doing well and hope to see them soon. I want to give them some hope. I can't give you a letter to take to them, but please give them this." She handed Marta a small pencil drawing of a butterfly. "They know how much I love butterflies, and maybe this will give them some reassurance that I will return. Someday I will fly back to them."

On Easter Monday, April 26, 1943, just before dawn, a green-clad SS officer unlocked the cell door and pulled Josette, still asleep, to her feet. "Come with me!" He pushed her out the door and down the corridor to the rear of the prison. She could faintly hear Marta and Agnes saying goodbye. "Adieu, mon amie."

A large crowd of men, women, and children gathered in the large yard as soldiers surrounded them with their barking dogs, rifles, and truncheons at the ready. In single file they climbed aboard three large trucks that sat one behind the other. Josette was pushed toward the back of the truck. There were no benches or seats so everyone sat on the rusty floor. Her truck contained more men than women and only a few children. She looked over the crowd to see if she recognized anyone, suspecting that most were Jews, with perhaps a few Communists. There were several nuns in their black habits and mantillas. The door was slammed shut. There was no light, just shadows. The man next to her asked if she knew where they are going and how long the drive might be.

Josette shrugged her shoulders. "I can only tell you that I was told the Jews are being sent to Drancy. I am guessing that if they drive directly there it will take about eight hours, but what difference does it make? We have all heard about the German concentration camps with their gas chambers. Let's pray that Drancy isn't one of them."

For the first few hours of their ride, her new-found companion was very talkative. He told her his name was Abel. His wife, two children, and he were Jews who lived in Paris. They were able to escape the massive German roundup of over thirteen thousand Jews, the Vel' d'Hiv', on July 16 and 17 of last year. The family made their way to Tarbes and stayed on a small farm. The Nazis, along with the French Vichy police, raided the property and found them hiding in the barn along with another Jewish family. The guards separated him from his wife and children. He spent two weeks at the detainment center in Lourdes with no word on their whereabouts. He wondered if they were all traveling to Drancy and what their fate would be. He paused, overcome with a sense of hopelessness.

"I hope I see them again." Josette took his hand and tried to comfort him. She shared with him the story of her arrest, the murder of Claude, and her separation from Marcel and Nicole.

She squeezed his hand. "We must stay strong. We will not let them break our spirit."

Only one stop was made. Josette heard gas filling the tanks. Suddenly the door opened and several bags of food were thrown in along with a large metal bucket. In the darkness she heard the commotion of people fighting for the food, not nearly enough to feed all the prisoners being transported. Abel placed a stale piece of bread and a small piece of apple on her lap. "Thank you, Abel. This bread is as hard as a stick and nothing to drink!" There was no way to tell time, and eventually Josette fell into a deep sleep. The thunderous sound of bombs startled her awake.

The truck pulled over and stopped just as they heard the bombs explode, rocking the truck from side to side. Josette had heard that Allied aircraft were bombing closer to Paris. The bombing moved into the distance, but the truck still sat. At last the truck jerked forward and moved back onto the roadway. Abel cleared his throat. "Those bombs were very close. I heard just yesterday that hundreds were killed on April 4 when the RAF bombed Boulogne-Billancourt only six miles from Paris."

Josette did not respond and sat in silence. She smelled excrement all around her in the enclosed space. She thought, *isn't anyone using the bucket?* Sometime later, she heard several of the Jewish men and women singing. She remembered that it sounded like a song her father sang to her when she was a child. He told her it was a song of faith and hopefulness.

The truck finally came to a stop and the rear doors swung open. Josette looked over the seated crowd and saw the spring twilight with the setting sun in the distance. The SS officers, with their dogs, rushed them out of the truck. They were separated into four groups: men, women, children, and the elderly, which included those who may have infirmities. Josette stood with a group of sixteen women including the three nuns. Crying and confused children looked back for their parents as they were led away, some calling out for their mothers. Parents called back to them, telling them not to worry, that they would see them soon. One mother broke from the group and rushed to her little boy. Guards quickly surrounded her and beat her with whips and clubs, leaving her motionless on the ground. No one dared to move to come to her aid. The guards ushered the hushed groups towards the barracks, the cries of children and the scuffing of shoes the only sounds in the still air.

As Josette walked along with the other women, she took in the Drancy transit camp which was once a beautiful suburban area of Paris. Now it was acre upon acre of barbed-wire fencing, watch towers, barracks, warehouses, and thousands of prisoners from the occupied territories. She wondered how many were detained here. As they continued to move down a long courtyard, she saw large groups of children being loaded into the same trucks that brought her group here from Lourdes. The SS showed no mercy. They whipped and beat the children, and a dog was biting a little girl's leg. Josette, bearing witness to the stories she heard of German inhumanity, now knew they were true. There were no boundaries to this cruelty.

The German guards led Josette's group to a small warehouse. As they entered they saw other women standing in rows of five, ten rows deep. With slaps and shoves, they were placed behind them. They slowly moved ahead to a long table where they stood to complete a registration form. Once completed, they moved to another table where the female guard handed them their gray striped Drancy uniform.

They were then instructed to move to an area where their heads were shaved. From there they were handed a small towel and were told to move to the showers. The Drancy uniforms were hung on hooks. The women removed their clothes and placed them in a large pile in the middle of the room. The showers were quick and cold. Josette stood next to the three nuns who endured the same humiliation. Once dressed, they moved outside and the guards directed them to another long metal barrack which would be their living space for a time uncertain. As she entered the facility, Josette realized there were too many women and not enough beds. She wondered where she would sleep.

Her group was separated into different areas. Each of the women in her area was handed a piece of paper with a number on it. Mattresses, with numbers painted on them, were lined up against the wall. Her mattress number was 1806. She crawled on top of it and thought of Claude and prayed that the Lord would watch over her children. *I must remain strong*, she said to herself. With nothing to eat or drink, she cried herself to sleep.

Fourteen
April, 1943

Now We Are Orphans

Marcel and Nicole were hiding in the small storage closet off of the apartment balcony. One small round window let shafts of sunlight break through. It had been a long and terrifying day. They heard soldiers' voices, their papa's shouts, a gunshot, and their maman's wails. They cried, held hands, dozed, and prayed. They drank the water and shared the bread and pastry placed in a bag on the shelf. Marcel remembered his maman's words, "If we are gone more than twelve hours, open the envelope and follow the directions."

Marcel took inventory of the items left for them. He found a small torchlight, a compass, a backpack full of clothes, and two rain coats. Although their minds were elsewhere, to pass the time they did cross-word puzzles, drew pictures, and played tic-tac-toe on the paper they found. Nicole wanted Marcel to tell her that everything would return to the way it was. She peppered him with questions: "Do you think the Germans shot Papa with their guns? Why was Maman crying? When will they come for us? Maybe they are at the hospital?" Her brother's quick, short answers did not satisfy her tormented curiosity.

When they had entered the closet, Marcel looked at the time on the clock and jotted down 8:10 a.m. on the envelope left for them by Josette. It was now 6:00. The children kept hoping they would hear their parents' voices and their footsteps on the stairs. They were alone, and could not fully comprehend what was happening. They just knew that they wanted their parents to return to them.

Marcel glanced at the clock. 7:30. The temptation to open the envelope got the best of him. He tore it open and read it aloud to Nicole:

"My beautiful children, if you are reading this, you know that we have a terrible situation that you must deal with. Marcel, I know that you are strong and will take care of your sister. As soon as it turns dark, walk to Monsieur Pierre's house. Take the back alleys and walk quickly. Papa and I have talked to Monsieur Pierre and Madam Lucinda and they said that if Papa and I were taken away by the Germans, they would see that you both are taken care of until we are able to return. Papa and I love you and we will all be together very soon."

The children watched the darkness descend through the small, round window, and a half hour later Marcel told Nicole that it was time to leave. He threw the backpack over his shoulder and Nicole held her pet giraffe. They moved down the steps, through the garden, and into the small alley behind their apartment. Marcel took one long last look over his shoulder in hopes that he would see Claude and Josette. Holding hands, the children traversed the empty alleys and back streets that took them to Pierre and Lucinda's house, where the lights were burning brightly in the windows. They walked up the stone steps to the front door. Marcel knocked gently. Pierre came to the door.

"Lucinda, come greet our visitors, Marcel and Nicole!" Lucinda rushed to the door and gave the children a gentle embrace. "Nicole, you look so pretty in your pink dress and black shoes!" Nicole looked down at her dress. "Thank you. Today we had our Easter concert that I was looking forward to." Pierre took Marcel's backpack. Pierre and Lucinda could see that the children were tired and frightened. Earlier in the day, several friends had contacted them to share a rumor that the Germans broke into the bakery, fatally shot Claude, and arrested Josette.

Lucinda gently touched Nicole's hand. "You must be hungry. Let's go into the kitchen and we will fix you something." The four sat at the round table and the children picked at their food while Pierre and Lucinda sipped their coffee. Pierre refilled their cups with water. "Since you are alone, I suspect that the German soldiers came to the bakery? Please tell us what has happened." As best as they could, the children told them what they heard: the bell ringing in the apartment, the shouts, the shot, the cries. "We had many conversations with your parents and we told them that if any danger came to them, we would be here for you."

Marcel and Nicole looked for reassurance that their parents would return. "When do you think we will see them again?" Nicole asked. Pierre and Lucinda realized that it was too soon to tell them that their father had died and their maman arrested.

In a soft voice, Lucinda answered, "I do not think you can see them now, but we must be patient. Pierre will go to the bakery tomorrow morning and find some clothes for you. I will see that you get ready for school tomorrow morning and will walk with you so I can speak to your teachers. Since my cousin left we have a spare bedroom. Pierre will also try to find out more information about your parents. We must be hopeful and you both must stay strong. You have endured a terrifying day. So let's get you ready for bed, and we will pray for the return of your parents."

The next morning Lucinda helped the children dress, and after their breakfast she walked them to school. Pierre accompanied them part of the way and then said goodbye. As he walked away, Lucinda called after him, "Don't forget the truck!" He headed to the bakery carrying Marcel's backpack. The door was ajar, and as he pushed it open, he saw the blood stain and a spent rifle cartridge on the floor. The size of the cartridge told him that Claude could not have survived such a wound. Pierre remembered when this bakery was busy with customers enjoying themselves over coffee and a sweet treat, but now it had become a place of death and despair.

He looked around the bakery and walked back to the room where Diop stayed. He noticed that most of his clothes and shoes were missing. Upstairs in the apartment he found the children's closet and filled the backpack with as many of their clothes and shoes that could fit. He feared the Germans might return, so he made haste. He closed and locked the bakery front door. Spying the truck parked along the curb and down the street from the bakery, he walked quickly to it and found his key. The truck stuttered, started then stalled. He tried again and the engine began to hum. He pulled out and headed back to his house, fully aware that he was driving a truck that now belonged to the Third Reich.

He organized the children's clothes and then walked over to Town Hall. He headed to the front desk where he found a soldier writing in a large notebook. Standing in front of the desk, he asked, "*Parlez-vous français?*" (Do you speak French?). The soldier dropped his pencil. "Yes, but not very well. What brings you to us?"

"I am trying to confirm the whereabouts of two of my former employees and was told that someone here may be able to enlighten me regarding their status. I have been told that one has been shot and the other arrested." The soldier opened the desk drawer and searched for the necessary form. "You may sit here and complete the information required. I will need to see your identity card." Pierre filled out the information requested, and handed the form and his card to the soldier. "Please take a seat in the waiting area. I will take this to my commanding officer."

The wait was much longer than expected. He heard his name called out and walked back to the front desk. A German officer was holding the form and spoke in textbook French with a German accent. "Monsieur Rabete, please follow me." Pierre followed the officer to a small corner office. The officer sat behind the desk and motioned to Pierre to sit in front of him. "You are requesting information concerning the whereabouts of a Claude and Josette Garmon? You are a former employer of theirs, is that correct?"

"Yes, that is correct. I am the previous owner of a bakery here in Lourdes and I sold the business to them. They are also close friends of mine. I am worried about them." The officer glared at Pierre. "I can tell you that Monsieur Garmon assaulted one of our soldiers and was shot and killed. Madame Garmon is being detained. As you are aware, she is a Jew and we are investigating her case. She is accused of aiding the Maquis. The charges include sabotage and conspiracy. She will be transported to our detainment center at Drancy. The bakery property now belongs to the Third Reich. I believe I have sufficiently answered your questions. You are dismissed."

That evening, following dinner and homework, the children sat on the sofa with Pierre and Lucinda. Earlier, Pierre told

Lucinda about his meeting with the German officer. They decided they needed to break this horrible news to the children.

Pierre reached for Marcel's hand and Lucinda pulled Nicole close. Pierre's voice was shaking. "This afternoon, I spoke with a German officer and asked him to tell me what he could about your parents. This breaks our hearts, and this is going to be difficult for you to hear, but I want to be honest with both of you. Your father was shot and killed by the Germans when you were hiding in the balcony closet. You told us you heard the shot and the cries. Your maman has been arrested. She is being held in the jail next to the Town Hall. They tell me they will be sending her to a camp near Paris called Drancy. We do not know when we will see her again."

Marcel sat in stunned silence. "Now we are orphans!" Nicole cried. "They killed Papa and took Maman away. We are alone. What will happen to us?"

Still stoic, Marcel embraced his sister. "Nicole, I will take care of you. We must pray that Maman will return to us. Monsieur Pierre, will we be able to stay with you and Madame Lucinda?"

"Yes, of course, Marcel. Please know that you are welcome here and we will care for you."

Fifteen
August, 1943

Marcel and Nicole
Find a New Home

Marta Lemerre walked along the Avenue de la Gare on a beautiful warm August morning in Lourdes. She was on her way to the Rabete's home to fulfill her promise to Josette. She passed the small coffee shop on the Place de Ladieu and knew, from Josette's directions, that she was close. Turning the corner, she saw ahead of her the house Josette had described. Marta climbed the steps and knocked. She waited but there was no answer. She knocked again and the door inched open. Lucinda gave Marta a hesitant bonjour. Marta politely explained that she had been detained with Josette and had a message from her to her children.

"Please, do come in." Lucinda took Marta into the parlor. "I will get the children and my husband."

Marta thought that she must choose her words carefully. She did not want to upset the children, and she understood how the Rabetes must feel with a complete stranger in their house. In a few minutes, Lucinda returned with Marcel and Nicole. Pierre, his shoulders stooped, took small hesitant steps with his cane as he walked over to greet Marta.

They all sat close to one another on the divan. The children were excited but anxious. Marcel held Nicole's hand. Marta stood and walked over to give the children a small hug. "My visit will be brief. I am bringing you a message from your maman. She told me all about both of you." She holds Marcel's hand.

"So you are Marcel," she said, and placing her other hand gently on Nicole's head, "and this is your sister, Nicole. Marcel, your maman told me that you will be thirteen, and Nicole, you are nine. She asked me to come find you and deliver to you a message from her. She knew that you were worried about her. We both were being held here in Lourdes by the German police. I was so blessed to have met her. What a wonderful, loving, and caring person she is. She wanted to write you both a letter explaining what happened to her, but the Germans would not allow it. She made me promise that I would visit with you and bring her message."

Marta reached inside her purse and pulled out the picture of the butterfly that Josette had given to her. "This is from your maman. She said that she loves butterflies and that she always told you that when you see a butterfly, you will know that she is sending you loving thoughts." Marta handed the pencil drawing to Nicole. She held it for a moment, kissed it, and showed it to Marcel.

"The Germans were about to transfer your maman to a camp near Paris called Drancy. She said to tell you that she is well and misses you so very much. She wanted you both to know that she thinks of you every day and prays that the Lord will watch over and protect you. She also asked that you keep praying for her and when this war is over, she will see you again. She said to be strong and watch over each other.

She knows that you miss your father and how difficult it must be for you to understand his death and your loss. She said to always remember your love for each other and to think of all the wonderful times your family shared. She knows that someday you will find again that love and happiness. She said never to forget her and to think of her and your father each day. She wants you to know how much she loves you."

Marcel could no longer hold back his tears. Nicole whimpered, "When will Maman come back to us?" Marta only shook her head. She looked to Lucinda.

"Thank you for coming, Marta. I know this was a difficult visit for you. You brought the children some hope."

"Josette also wanted me to thank you, Lucinda and Pierre, for caring for her children." Marta reached in her large purse and handed Marcel and Nicole each a small box.

"I have some chocolate for you. Your maman said you both liked vanilla butter cream." Lucinda wiped the children's tears from their faces with her handkerchief.

"*Merci beaucoup* (thank you very much), Madame Marta." Marta bid everyone a goodbye and showed herself to the door.

"Well that was a surprise and an unexpected visit!" Lucinda exclaimed, trying to cheer the children. "It was so nice of her to come to see you. Now we know where the Germans are sending your maman. Children, it may be some time before your maman returns, but you must remain strong and remember how much she loves you. Soon this war will be over and you will be reunited with her."

Pierre and Lucinda continued to watch over the children, trying to keep them occupied and happy. They heard that their school may not open. They soon came to the realization that they couldn't pretend to be parents to two active children. Now in their mid-seventies, and dealing with multiple health problems, they were having difficulty taking care of themselves, let alone two young children. With two more mouths to feed, their ration cards were not enough for all four, and food was in short supply throughout all of France, with most of the agricultural production being shipped to Germany. Lucinda spent most of her day standing in long lines waiting for a small amount of meat and dairy products. The harsh reality was that if it were not for the generosity of their friends and neighbors, they would be starving.

The children were not happy. Lucinda and Pierre noticed changes in their behaviors and attitudes. They were bored, quick to anger, and it was difficult for Lucinda and Pierre to interact with them. They both were quiet and withdrawn. Pierre knew that Marcel liked to play chess, so often they sat together at the chess board. Marcel made a friend with a younger boy who lived nearby, and occasionally they played soccer together. Nicole had not met any young girls her age, and although she liked to join Lucinda in the shopping queues, there was not much else to keep her occupied. Lucinda read a children's book to her most evenings, but when the book was finished, Nicole always asked, "When is my maman coming back and where will we live?"

Summer was quickly passing, and Pierre and Lucinda had had many discussions about the children and how they would continue to care for them. One evening, after the children were in bed, they sat in the kitchen sipping their cups of tea. Pierre placed his cup on the table and looked at Lucinda.

"I think it is time to see if Mother Anne Marie will keep the children at the orphanage. I know we both realize and understand that we are no longer physically or mentally capable of caring for Marcel and Nicole. We can see that they are unhappy here. If the Allies land, as rumored, our situation here will only grow worse, and who knows how long this war will continue. We are not their family, and as far as I know, they have no family. There are no uncles, aunts, or cousins who can care for them."

Lucinda touched Pierre's hand. "Yes, I agree, and it breaks my heart, but it is something that must happen. I remember thinking and hoping when Nicole cried out, 'Now we are orphans!' that Josette would be released and return to them. The reality is that she may never return from the German camps. We know about the gas chambers and, God forbid, I fear that might be her fate." Lucinda began to cry.

Pierre was teary-eyed as well. "I will get a message to Mother and see what kind of response we get. She knows the children and was close to Claude and Josette. She will understand our circumstances. My heart breaks when I think about the children's future. The Germans created this inhumanity. How much longer will it last?"

One evening after sunset, there was a knock on their door. Lucinda hurried to open it. She stepped out onto the porch and looked in all directions but saw no one. She then noticed a small envelope lying near her door mat. She picked it up and rushed in to show it to Pierre. "Here, you open it." Inside, Pierre found a small note on an index card. He read aloud, "*Within the next two nights, expect a visitor to knock on your door.*" It was signed by Mother Anne Marie.

On a Sunday evening in September, the children were sleeping as Lucinda and Pierre looked out their large picture window at the full moon rising over the mountains. They heard a quick knock on the door. Pierre opened it and almost fell backward when he saw Diop. "*Mon Dieu! Entrez! Entrez!*" (My God! Come in! Come in!). Lucinda hastened over to Diop and embraced him. They gathered around the kitchen table as Lucinda heated a pot of coffee.

Pierre leaned forward and spoke softly. "Diop, the children are fast asleep. It is so good to see you. We had heard rumors that you joined the Resistance and that you were wounded in one of their attacks. You are looking well. I am sure you heard about Claude being murdered by the Germans and Josette's arrest. Tell us what you can about your activities. Did Mother send you here?"

Diop told them that he knew about Claude and Josette. "I am still grieving for them. They were family and such good, loving people. I will forever miss them." He paused.

"I am thankful that my wound was a minor one and I only have a bit of soreness. That was my first firefight. My friend René was killed along with another member of my group. I am thankful that I survived."

Diop told them a bit more about his Resistance activities but in very vague terms. "Yes, Mother Anne Marie is good friends with my commander, Colonel Emile Dumond. I carried messages from him to Mother. On my last visit she asked if I would come to see you and bring Marcel and Nicole to the orphanage."

Pierre and Lucinda told Diop about their health problems, financial setbacks, and their concern about the children's future. "It breaks our hearts to see them leave us, Diop," Lucinda said, "but it is the correct decision. Mother's orphanage is our only option. We remain hopeful that after the war is over Josette will find her way back to them."

The three agreed that Diop would spend the night and take them to the orphanage in the morning. Pierre insisted that Diop transport the children in the bakery truck. "I have no further use for the truck. Perhaps Mother may need it, or your Resistance group. Tell your commander to fill it with explosives and park it in front of one of the hotels the Nazis have taken over here in Lourdes."

Diop laughed at that suggestion and expressed concern that the Germans may have set up road blocks on the route between

Lourdes and Tarbes that would endanger them. Pierre went over to the kitchen cabinet and found an old dusty map. "Here Diop, you can see here that there is an old logging road that runs through the forest for at least eight miles. That is the route you should take. It would be much safer and few even know it exists."

The following morning Pierre, Lucinda, and Diop were gathered in the kitchen when Marcel and Nicole entered from their bedroom. They ran over to Diop and enfolded him in a loving embrace. Nicole began to cry. "Did you know that the Germans killed our Papa and arrested Maman?" Diop hugged her to him. "Yes, I have known for a while. I am so sorry for both of you. You know that I loved them very much."

The children wanted to know all about Diop's absence and his travels. Diop was reluctant to tell them too much about his Resistance activities. He did tell them about his wound and the death of René at the Pau airfield. Marcel asked when the war with Germany would be over. Diop only shook his head. "Marcel, I wish I knew. My main concern is to help keep you and Nicole safe."

Lucinda had prepared a warm meal of scrambled eggs and sausage. The five sat at the table, and Lucinda spoke in a halting voice as she looked at the children. "We have something very important to discuss with you and that is why Diop is here." Lucinda took a deep breath.

"You know that we have tried to care for you both as best we could, but we have reached the age where we are having difficulty responding to your needs. We have decided that you would be most happy and very well cared for if you lived with Mother Anne Marie at the orphanage. There is a school, and you can make friends with children your age."

Diop looked at Marcel. "As you know from our deliveries there, the orphanage is located in one of the most beautiful parts of France. You and Nicole will enjoy the mountains, rivers, sheep, chickens, and cows. There is a lovely garden and a sports field. It is not as dangerous there, but you will see some German soldiers from time to time. I know, Marcel, that you liked watching the children on the playground and soccer field. Nicole, the orphanage has a library and a children's choir. I think you both will like it there, and Mother Anne Marie is very kind and caring."

The children listened to Lucinda and Diop intently, trying to comprehend the changes that were about to happen.

"We will finish breakfast and gather your belongings," Diop continued. "Pierre said that I can have the truck, so I will take you there. We can drive through the forest and be there before dinner. Mother is expecting us. Shall we get ready to go?" The children looked back and forth at the adults, unsure of what to think or feel but wanting to trust them. Nicole looked at Marcel, who nodded yes. Nicole nodded yes, too.

"All will be well," Pierre said.

After breakfast, Lucinda helped the children fill their rucksacks. She and Pierre hugged them tightly and waved goodbye as they followed Diop to the truck. Lucinda wiped her eyes. "Another chapter begins for them, Pierre. I only hope it will have a happy ending."

The truck made its way along the rocky, muddy path through the dense forest and then onto the main highway. The ride was uneventful and they enjoyed Diop's stories and company. As the afternoon retreated into early evening, the gates of the orphanage came into view. Diop pulled up to the main entrance, parked on the grass, and the three walked up to the door carrying their rucksacks. They rang the bell and were greeted by a young teenage girl. Diop introduced himself and the children. The girl told them to take a seat in the office while she went to find Mother.

All three stood as Mother Anne Marie entered the office. She warmly embraced them and gave each a quick kiss on each cheek. "Oh my, Marcel, how you have grown since the last time I saw you! Please be seated so we can chat and I can tell you about the orphanage. Diop, thank you for bringing the children to me. I don't want to delay your trip back to your camp. I have a box here for you. You will need it for your next trip to visit Brother Jerome at the abbey in Urt."

Diop turned to the children. "Remember that I love both of you and you will see me from time to time. I will stop by to visit and check on you whenever I can." He gave each a warm hug, picked up the box, and headed to the front door. "Bon soir, mes amis. *Vous allez me manquer*" (I will miss you).

Sixteen
September, 1943

Josette Arrives at Auschwitz

Josette's last several months at Drancy were horrific. Despite the beatings, the lack of food, and twelve-hour work days, she tried to remain hopeful. Following her 4 a.m. roll call each morning, she was assigned to work with tailors as they fabricated the prison uniforms. Her job was to cut the fabric and stitch hems on prison dress uniforms. Mostly, they were one-size-fits-all. She was not allowed to sit, so she worked standing at a large table with nine other French women prisoners. It was difficult, tedious, manual labor.

The women shared stories and heard dreadful news from newly-arrived prisoners concerning the death camps in Poland. They were often whipped, slapped, kicked, or hit by their guards for not working fast enough. As more prisoners arrived, their output quotas were increased with no additional help. If someone fainted, they were kicked until they could get on their feet. If someone tried to help, they were whipped. At the end of each day, Josette's hands were swollen and she could hardly move her fingers. For six days a week her routine was always the same. Sundays afforded a modicum of rest. There was a small group of Catholic women who gathered and recited prayers together. There was also a brief amount of time to walk outside and enjoy the hot summer weather. The prisoners were also expected to clean the barracks and wait in a long line to take their weekly shower.

At Monday morning roll call, the women in Josette's confinement area were told that several would be leaving Drancy that afternoon. They were told that if their names appeared on the list posted, they must assemble in the courtyard outside their barrack at twelve noon. Josette's name was on the list, and at noon she stood in the crowded courtyard in the hot sun with hundreds of other women, some children, and a few elderly men scattered about.

A line of trucks drove toward them as they were pushed and shoved through the open doors. No one knew what the destination would be, but there were rumors that they were going to the Drancy rail station and from there to a Nazi death camp in Poland. It was a quick ride as the trucks pulled up to a large open area next to a line of cattle cars and unloaded their prisoners. The crowd was surrounded by German SS with their barking dogs as they were pushed toward the waiting rail cars.

Josette moved along to one of the cattle cars and entered through its sliding doors. She was one of the last to enter, and she guessed that there were at least a hundred people crowded into this rail car that smelled of animal waste encrusted on the rough wooden floors. She moved to the side wall and sat in the corner which provided a bit more space. She pulled her knees up against her chest as the others tripped and fell over her. An elderly man took a seat on one side of her along with a mother holding a baby on the other side. The women in front of her leaned back against her legs. Just before the doors were slammed shut, an SS soldier threw in a potato sack full of apples and a large wooden bucket. Having waited for hours in the stifling heat, the train began its journey.

Day after day the crowd yelled, cried, pushed, and shoved each other, and sometimes they sang patriotic French songs. They took turns moving toward the bucket full of urine and excrement. The word circulated that several in the crowd had died. The man next to her was mostly silent and prayerful. He took turns with Josette holding the woman's young child so she could nap and doze. The young mother was breast-feeding the infant, and the baby seemed content in spite of the harsh conditions. She told Josette that her name was Celina and she was a school teacher in Paris, but lost her position because of her Jewish mother. Her husband was a French soldier and was captured at the beginning of the war. She had received a letter from him from a German labor camp where they mined coal. Sadly, her husband had never seen the beautiful little girl they named Camille. Celina's beautiful green eyes reminded Josette of Nicole as she told Celina all about her once-happy life in Lourdes.

The man next to her became more talkative, and Josette was surprised to hear that he was a Catholic priest and a member of the Jesuits. He was imprisoned for forging documents for the Resistance. His name was Father Gabriel. Josette and the priest prayed together in quiet voices. He was an encyclopedia of stories about the saints, his favorites were St. Ignatius and St. Anthony. He also told her about a priest who gave up his life for another prisoner at Auschwitz just two years ago, in 1941, and may someday become a saint. His name was Father Maximilian Kolbe. As Father Gabriel told the story, he attracted the attention of several other women seated around him. He told them that the priest was Polish and a Franciscan friar who volunteered to die in place of a stranger.

Father Gabriel's voice got a little louder. "From what I have been told about Father Kolbe, he was sent to Auschwitz for hiding Jews. The Nazis have a starvation bunker. For even the most minor infraction, a prisoner may be sent there to die. No food or water and death comes quickly. The Nazi guards selected ten prisoners to be starved to death. Although he was not among the ten selected, a stranger in his group was. As the Nazis were carrying him away, the man yelled out, 'My poor wife and children need me!' Father Kolbe approached the guards and told them to take him instead. The guards dropped the man and took Kolbe. As St. John tells us, "No greater love than this that a man lays down his life for another." Many of the women began to cry.

It was the beginning of the third day in the cattle car. The bag of apples was passed around and eaten on the first day. Since then, there had been no food or water. There was no ventilation and the prisoners sat in shadows and darkness. Everyone seemed to agree that Auschwitz was their destination. Stories were shared about its horror. They talked about the gas chambers, starvation, beatings, disease, and executions. The Nazis had created a hell on earth.

Josette still had hope and tried to remain mentally strong. She fixated on her return to Marcel and Nicole. As she dozed, the train began to slow and blew its whistle. Everyone was alert and frightened and prayed for survival. Josette asked Father Gabriel for his blessing as she made the sign of the cross.

The train jerked to a stop, and within a few minutes the doors opened and they were faced by SS guards and their dogs. Josette stepped over the bodies of three women and a man as she was pushed out of the cattle car. Everyone gathered next to the rail station. Josette took in the beautiful blue sky and mid-day sun, consciously avoiding the pile of dead bodies lying on the platform. The prisoners were separated into various groups: young women, women with children, older women, men, and the elderly.

Josette saw the camp in the distance and the sign on the front of the rail station: *Auschwitz*. The stark realization of her fate descended on her like a pall. The German guards told them to walk toward the large sign at the entrance: *Arbeit Macht Frei*. Josette asked if anyone could translate the sign. "Work Sets You Free," said the French woman walking next to her, and bitterly laughed. "Here, only death will set you free."

The prisoners were pushed and herded toward a large metal building. The women with children and the group of elderly were separated from the others and moved to the left in the direction of another building spewing dark smoke. As the remaining men and women entered the building they were moved toward a series of partitions, each one containing several SS soldiers seated at a long table. On each side of the table were Nazi swastika flags. Josette moved toward one of the chairs and sat in front of a young soldier. He handed her a registration form to complete. When asked to state her occupation, she wrote "artist—painter of portraits."

She kept the registration form and was told to move to the next partition. The soldier had written the number 440817 at the top of her form. At the next partition everyone was being tattooed. The soldier pulled up the sleeve of her Drancy uniform and rubbed her left inner arm, just below the elbow, with a dirty rag he touched to a bottle of alcohol. He injected ink into the needle, and with harsh strokes tattooed the registration number on her arm. Josette, now just a number among thousands of others, winced in pain as she moved to the next station. At the next table she had her head shaved. She then moved to an enclosed dressing room where she was stripped of her clothes, shaved of all body hair, and given a striped Auschwitz uniform with the yellow Star of David stitched on the front. She stumbled into her mismatched shoes, each a different size.

Josette was moved along with a large group of women to a warehouse. As she entered, she saw a long stretch of wooden partitions enclosing raised platforms, which would be their sleeping space. The prisoners were pushed along until they reached their designated spot where four prisoners would sleep. The Germans called the sleeping space the *buk*. Behind the warehouse there was a bathhouse with cold showers, a latrine with wooden planks over a ditch, and equipment for disinfecting clothing.

The evening meal was at 6 p.m. and was placed on a long table at the back of the warehouse. The women formed a line and moved toward the table where they were handed a small tin tray. On this day, each received a piece of moldy bread, a small piece of cheese, a tiny sausage along with a cup of brown water.

An hour later there was a roll call. Josette stood in front of her sleeping space as two SS officers walked along each line with their clipboards. They looked at the extended arms and checked off each prisoner's number. Several were flogged for not moving fast enough. When Josette's officer checked her number, he asked her to step forward. He looked at her and said, "Stand here and don't move. When I complete my count, I will be back for you."

Josette trembled as she watched him walk along the row of women and then abruptly turn and walk back to her. "Follow me." All of the women watched as Josette walked behind the SS guard and through the exit door. Several women whispered, "She is going to be gassed!" As Josette and the guard entered a small building, she was shaking and wondering what type of punishment awaited her.

The SS soldier handed an officer seated at a desk a sheet of paper, then turned, saluted, and left the building. The officer pointed her to the chair in front of his desk. In halting French he spoke. "Be seated. So you are 440817. Your registration indicates that you are an artist, a painter of portraits. Is that correct?" Josette nodded. The officer told Josette to tell him about her portrait-painting experience. "I have painted portraits, mainly of friends and family. I also paint landscapes, flowers, mountain scenes, and other pictures of nature, including animals."

He reached under his desk and pulled out a large sheet of paper and placed it in front of her. He handed her a sharp pointed pencil and a framed picture of a German officer. "This is a photograph of our Kommandant, Rudolf Hoss. I will give you thirty minutes to draw a pencil portrait of his face. I want to see how good you really are. I will be back. There is a guard just outside."

Josette was still shaking and hoped she could steady her hand. She studied the black and white photograph and knew thirty minutes was not enough time as she looked at the large clock on the wall. She also knew that she must be successful. She looked at the photo and studied the prominent features of his face: his wide nose, deep eye sockets, large ears, and skinny neck. As she drew she tried to compare the length of his face with the width and used her pencil as a ruler. The image on the photograph quickly took shape on her paper. Her normal style for a portrait was slow and meticulous, but not this evening. After thirty-five minutes, the officer returned and looked over her shoulder as she finished the strokes on his eyebrows. She turned to look at him. "I did my best, but thirty minutes was not enough time."

The officer took the paper and examined it. "I am impressed. I was an art teacher at a secondary school in Berlin, and I paint as well. I believe you will be hearing from our Kommandant." He called in the guard who pushed her back to the warehouse.

As she climbed into her bunk, the woman above her asked what the guards wanted. "They wanted me to draw a picture."

"Don't lie to me," the woman exclaimed with a dismissive taunt.

Seventeen
October, 1943

Life at the Orphanage

At the Orphanage of St. Stephen, Mother Anne Marie was sitting between Marcel and Nicole on a couch in her office. She touched their hands.

"I know it was very difficult for Pierre and Lucinda to say good-bye to you. I am so sorry about the death of your father and the arrest of your mother. There is nothing I can do to take away your hurt, but know that I will be here for both of you. I am very happy that you are now with us, but I want to be completely honest with you. The war continues and we never know when we, or our children here, will be in danger. Let me tell you what lies ahead for you.

"Unfortunately, you will be separated. The boys and girls cannot live together. Because of our limited resources, you will attend the same school, so you will see each other there. Marcel, you will be entered into our eighth grade, and Nicole, you will be in our fourth grade. Our classes are small. Marcel, you will take English language lessons along with mathematics, world history, French grammar, and religion classes. Nicole, you will take mathematics, geography, French grammar, penmanship, and religion classes. Both of you will also take music lessons, and we have a children's choir. You both will be very busy. School will start next week."

Mother had the children's full attention. Nicole asked, "Where will I sleep and eat?" Mother walked over to a campus map hanging on the wall.

"Nicole, that is an excellent question. Please step over here and I will show you your new home. As you can see we have nine separate buildings. We are here in the main office building with two buildings on each side of us. One is our chapel and the other is our school. We have four separate dormitories for our children, two for boys and two for girls. They have bathrooms and showers. Behind the school is the convent where the sisters live, and next to that is our dining hall. You will be doing a lot of walking! Our children here are separated by gender and age. Nicole, you will be in a dormitory with girls between the ages of five to twelve, and Marcel, you will be with boys ages thirteen to eighteen. Do you have any other questions?"

"What about clothes?" asked Marcel. "Do we have to wear a uniform?"

Mother looked at their rucksacks. "It looks like Lucinda sent you with some clothes. Don't worry, Marcel. Because of the donations from our friends, we have clothes for you in all sizes. During the school day, you will wear a uniform. In your dormitory you will have an assigned locker for your clothes and shoes." Mother paused.

"There is one very important thing you must not forget," she continued. "We have had lorries pull up here with German soldiers who make unannounced searches of all of our buildings. If or when that happens, you must freeze wherever you are. If they approach you, remain silent and point them toward your teacher or your dormitory sister or brother."

Marcel was confused. "I don't understand what you mean when you say we will have a dormitory sister or brother."

"We have sisters living here who are members of our order, the Sisters of Love and Charity," Mother explained. "Each day one sister will stay in each of the girls' dormitories to look after and assist them. We also have friars here from their abbey who look after the boys in their dormitories. These are your dormitory brothers and sisters. On occasion they will also be your teachers. Do you both understand?"

"I think so," said Marcel. Nicole looked anxiously at her brother. Mother knelt down and took Nicole's hands in hers.

"There is nothing I can say to take away your hurt, but know that I will be here for you whenever you need me. Little by little, you will let go of this terrible loss of your parents, but never the love for your maman and papa. That love and their memories will always be with you." She stood in front of them.

"Remember that your papa is in heaven with Jesus and he is looking after you. Stay seated for a moment. Let me go and find someone to take you to your dormitories so you can meet your new friends."

In short order Mother entered the room with a sister following her. "Sister Aubree, please welcome two new children to our home, Marcel and Nicole." Sister Aubree, a tall, slender nun with large brown eyes, shook Marcel's hand and gave Nicole a small hug. Mother picked up their rucksacks and handed them to the children. "Sister Aubree is the principal of our school. She will take you to your new living area. Sister, after you help the children settle in, please come back to my office for a brief meeting."

Within the hour, Sister Aubree gently tapped on Mother's open door. Mother looked up from a stack of papers. "Please come in. Let's move to the conference table. Did it go well with the children?"

Sister Aubree found a chair next to Mother. "They were quiet. I introduced them to several of the boys and girls who were in their rooms and showed them their lockers and bath facilities. I could tell they both were nervous, but as they settle in they will adjust to their new life here. The first few days are always the most difficult."

Mother nodded, then handed Sister Aubree a file. "We need to discuss the four Jewish children hiding here. We just received a brother and sister last week. I believe they are eight and ten years old. We also have the two older boys, ages fifteen and seventeen. They arrived about three weeks ago. I have requested birth and baptismal certificates for all of them. Once those documents are received, the older boys will be ready for their trek across the Pyrénées. Since all four have Jewish names, I created new Christian identities for them.

"Sister Agatha is working to instill in them their new identities and their cover stories. They must quickly memorize their new names, their new places of birth, and where they lived. They, like all the others we have saved, will become new persons. The older boys understand the reason and the urgency, but it is always much more difficult with the younger children. If the Germans surprise us, we must be ready. Concerning Marcel and Nicole, they have Christian names, so there is no need to change their identities nor hide them. However, we will need to erase their Jewish heritage. I will obtain new documents for them from Brother Jerome."

Sister Aubree leafed through the file. "I will begin work on their file cards and continue to list their real identities along with their false identifications, and I will need to place their fingerprints in their file before I hide them. Is there anything else?"

Mother opened her desk drawer and retrieved another file. "Just to let you know, here is the file on the Allard twins, Dion and Darcy. I have a couple arriving next Saturday morning who want to foster them. They are very excited to start a family with them. They are in their early thirties and have no children. Please be sure the twins are packed and ready to go. The foster parents will also need the children's birth and baptismal certificates. Also, since Dion was one of our altar boys, let's see if Marcel would like to replace him."

On the last two Saturday mornings after breakfast, Marcel and Nicole met on a bench near the sports field. They sat next to a weathered statue of an angel with a lost wing. They greeted each other with hugs, and Marcel repeated his ritual of lifting Nicole's hand and kissing the birthmark on the third finger of her left hand. On this day, Marcel asked Nicole how she liked her studies and her new friends. "My classes are fine. I really like the mathematics. My teacher, Sister Marion, tells us that she loves us and is ready to help if there is something we don't understand. One girl I really like sleeps next to me. Her name is Ruth. She is my age. Her parents died when Paris was attacked by the airplanes. She told me a secret. She said that her parents were Jewish and her last name was Abelman, but the sisters here changed it to Fabron, so it sounds more French and not Jewish. They did that to help hide her from the Germans. If the Germans find any Jewish people here at the orphanage, they will be arrested. She said I had to swear not to tell anyone, but Marcel, I know you can keep a secret."

Marcel squeezed her hand. "You know I will not tell anyone. I have heard some of the same stories from several of the boys in my dormitory.

"I am sad today. This afternoon, one of my friends, Dion, is leaving along with his twin sister, Darcy. They will be living with foster parents in Semeac, a town not far from here. It seems that when I meet someone I really like, he leaves. He liked soccer and we played chess."

Nicole looked intently at her brother. "Marcel, I hope this orphanage is a safe place for us. If the Germans come, what will happen to us? I miss Maman and Papa and our home in Lourdes. When will Maman return to us?"

Eighteen
November, 1943

Josette's Final Days

Josette's life in Auschwitz knew no boundaries for cruelty and inhumanity. Each day she was a witness to death and torture and the smell of smoke from the crematoriums. A woman was called out at evening roll call for losing the yellow star on her uniform. A German guard dragged in a metal frame and forced her to lean over it. He then pulled down her uniform and began striking her bare back with his cane until she fainted. Her blood stained the floor. Josette and two others were forced to remove it with dirty rags.

Josette was barely recognizable—a once beautiful woman had become more bone than skin. The nights in the brick blockhouse were getting colder and there were few blankets and not enough heat. Rats, mice, lice, and fleas were her bedfellows. Night after night her dinner was always the same: rotted potato soup and stale bread.

Each Sunday, there were once-a-week showers in cold water. Also on Sunday, the prisoners were allowed to write to their families, but they were not allowed to receive mail. The prisoners knew that the German SS read their letters and that their mail was censored. Josette wrote letters every Sunday to Pierre and Lucinda hoping that the children would be told that she was alive and "working" for the Germans at their "camp" in Poland. She knew that if she said anything about beatings, torture, or cremations, the letter would be thrown away, and that would put an end to her letter-writing and bring on additional punishment. She, along with several of her fellow inmates, formed a pact concerning their letters to family, relatives, or friends. They shared and then carefully hid addresses, so if one in their group died, someone would write an obscure message to notify the designated family or friends.

Following roll call one Sunday evening, Josette and two other inmates were pushed out of line and told to follow the SS guard to a small table at the back of the blockhouse. He smiled at the three. "A new assignment for you beginning tomorrow morning. You will begin working at the Kanada warehouse. I will take you over at 5 a.m. Be standing here when I arrive."

On the following morning the women waited at the table. They knew about the Kanada warehouse. Kanada held the stolen belongings of arriving Jews. Since many of the Jews had been told they would be "resettled," they were allowed to bring personal belongings of up to one hundred pounds for their trip to Auschwitz. The name Kanada was created by the Auschwitz inmates, who viewed Canada as a land of riches and wealth.

The SS guard walked them over to the first of three Kanada warehouses where most of the inmate workers were women. Josette walked past mounds of bodies waiting to be moved to the crematoriums as she recited a quick prayer. She was given her work assignment by a nasty German Jewish woman who became her supervisor. Her task, along with several other inmates, was to sort through mountains of clothing and create separate piles of men, women, and children's clothing. Once assorted, the clothes were to be labeled "Good," "Better," "Best," and "Worst." There was also a pile to be labeled "Minor Repair."

Compared to the work assigned to other inmates in Josette's blockhouse, Kanada did have some benefits. For inmates who wanted to take the risk, food and candy they found could be secreted back to other inmates, along with some occasional medications. From time to time a small diamond, ruby, or other gemstone surfaced and was used for bartering purposes.

Josette stood on her feet for twelve long hours. She was thankful that she didn't have to labor outdoors in the gravel pits and lumber yards, especially during the onset of the colder months. At midday the workers were given a foul-tasting meat cake and some hard potatoes.

One Sunday evening at roll call, she was pulled out of line and marched to the back of the blockhouse by an SS guard. She saw the rear door open and the German officer who asked her to draw the portrait entered and walked over to her. He handed her a note written in French and stood close as she read it: *Obersturmbannfuhrer Rudolf Höss, the Kommandant of Auschwitz, will meet with you tomorrow morning at 8 a.m. in his office.*

The officer saw her shaking hand and spoke to her in broken French. "Report to Kanada at your assigned time and I will meet you there and take you to the office of our *Kommandant.* There is no need to be concerned. He has a special project for you."

At 7:30 the following morning, Josette was busy sorting children's clothes. She thought about all of the beautiful children who had worn these clothes. How was it possible that she could be standing here touching the clothing of children whom she knew had suffered death in the crematoriums? The enormity of the death count shocked her mind, and she wondered how there could be so much inhumanity, only to please a madman.

Wrapped deep in thought, she was startled by a tap on her shoulder. She turned to see the SS officer standing next to her. "Come with me."

He led the way as they left Kanada and walked past many warehouse buildings until they arrived at a small row of large villas. They walked up a long sidewalk to the front door of a large brick and stone home. Two armed soldiers stood guard at the door. Josette's guide saluted both and handed one a note card. The soldier read the card, then opened the door. The SS officer motioned for her to follow him inside.

Josette stood close to the SS officer as she took in the beauty of the home: wooden bookcases, antique corner cabinets filled with crystal figures, leather sofas and chairs, beautiful draperies. *What beauty*, she thought, *all stolen from the Jews*. The officer looked at her frail body in her wrinkled, smelly uniform.

"The reason you are here is to paint the portrait of *Kommandant* Höss. He is in charge of the entire Auschwitz facility. He will sit for you this morning for no more than ninety minutes unless an emergency develops. While he poses, he may also be handling telephone calls and conducting other business. I have assorted brushes and oil paints of various colors ready for you. Follow me to the sun porch."

He handed her a white dress. "Put this on now before he enters. He will be seated on a small stage near the rear entrance. I think this sunny day will work for you. The more light the better. Remember, do not speak to him unless he speaks to you. I will be next to you and act as your interpreter."

Josette couldn't believe that she had been tasked to paint the portrait of the most feared person in all of Auschwitz. Promptly at 8:00 Rudolf Höss entered and was saluted by the SS officers in the room. He took his seat on a straight-backed chair and straightened his uniform which was bedecked with an array of medals. Josette was aware of his glaring look and menacing stare as she walked toward him. He squirmed uncomfortably as he positioned himself firmly against the back of the chair. He spoke in a strong, deep voice. "Only paint from the chest up."

The SS interpreter translated. Josette gave a nod and walked back to her work table. She lightly sketched in pencil on the large canvas. His facial features began to appear, the ones she remembered from the photo she sketched some weeks ago: his large nose, deep eye sockets, bushy brown eyebrows, large ears, and thin neck. Once his face was outlined she began to blend the paint colors to match his skin color and texture. She moved on to his eyes and hair color.

As she concentrated, she heard his phone ring. Höss jumped up and walked over to his phone which sat on a small desk near her table. He spoke in a hushed voice and then yelled, "Everyone out of here! Hitler and Eichmann are coming on the line!"

The SS officer wrapped his large, meaty hand around her bony arm and led her through the house to the front porch. Almost an hour later, Höss opened the door and called the SS officers over to talk with him. After a quiet conversation, Josette's guard walked her back, in silence, to the Kanada warehouse. He waited at the warehouse door as she took off her white dress and handed it to him. "I am not sure when you will complete his portrait. I will move the canvas to a safe place. When he is ready, I will come back for you."

Josette returned to her work routine in the Kanada warehouse. A few days after her return to sorting clothes, she felt unwell and began to cough. Each day she felt worse and the pain increased. A week into her coughing, she woke with a temperature and red spots on her body. She was dizzy with chills and a headache. At roll call she could hardly stand. She told the officer that she was unable to work on this day. To her surprise, he told her to return to her mattress. Her body ached and her cough worsened. At the end of the workday, Josette's bunkmates returned to find her in great pain and coughing blood. She looked at Viviane, the woman who slept next to her. "Don't get near me. I think I may have typhus. Tonight I will sleep on the floor."

She was too sick to stand for evening roll call and stayed in her bunk. The guard called out her number and Viviane stepped forward. "That is the number of my companion, Josette. She is very sick and is unable to leave her bed. Is it possible to take her to the camp hospital?" The guard looked at his sheet and made a notation. He pushed Viviane back in line with his baton. "I made note of her sickness. Tomorrow I will have a medical attendant look at her."

Just before the lights-out siren, Viviane insisted that Josette sleep on their mattress while she crowded in with two of the other women. The women in her group tried to make Josette comfortable. Her fever had spiked and she was confused. She told them that her children were lying next to her and she saw angels sitting on their shoulders. As the lights went out the women heard her speaking in a delirious whisper as the cold night settled in.

The following morning, on Friday, November 19, 1943, at 4:30 a.m., the block guard sounded the wake-up gong. The women knew they had to move quickly to wash and use the latrines. As she stumbled out of bed, Viviane stopped to check on Josette. She looked into eyes that were open, but from which no sight emanated. She gently shook Josette's shoulder. There was no movement and she knew that Josette had passed. Hands covering her face, through tears of grief, Viviane knelt and prayed, "May the souls of the faithful departed, through the mercy of God, rest in peace."

Nineteen
December, 1943

Nicole's Adoption

Every Friday, Pierre stopped by the postal center not far from his house. The mail was spotty at best and controlled by the Germans. For the past several weeks he and Lucinda were surprised to receive letters from Josette meant to be forwarded to Marcel and Nicole. They were always anxious to see what Josette had to tell the children. On occasion she attached a note just for Pierre and Lucinda. Her letters were brief. She always told the children how much she missed them and how her heart broke because they were not together. She mentioned the choir that she belonged to and how they sang to the German soldiers on Sunday afternoons. She told them about Kanada and her work there sorting children's clothes. In her last letter she mentioned that she was going to paint a portrait of the camp *Kommandant*. She also mentioned in her last note to Pierre and Lucinda that she was not feeling well and had developed a bad cough.

On this particular Friday, Pierre picked up his mail and noticed that one envelope was identical to the ones used by Josette, but the handwriting was different. As soon as he arrived home, he showed the envelope to Lucinda. "It appears that someone else has decided to write to us." Pierre handed the envelope to Lucinda. A neatly written note in pencil was inside.

With great sadness, I am informing you that Josette is no longer with us. She traveled on angel's wings to visit our Heavenly Father on November 19. She died from typhus at Auschwitz.
Her friend, Viviane

Lucinda let the note fall from her hands. "Oh, Pierre, this is the note Josette warned us about," she said, wiping tears from her face. "We continue to hear about the horror of the German concentration camps, but we do not want to believe it. And yet, here it is. Why did Josette have to suffer and die at the hands of these German monsters? She was such a good person and a loving mother. Another sorrowful conversation the children will have to endure. I know they were hopeful that their mother would return to them, but now they truly are orphans."

Pierre and Lucinda asked one of their relatives to drive them to visit Marcel and Nicole at the orphanage, usually twice a month. It was a quick ride of twenty kilometers. Their visit was usually brief, and Mother preferred visits on Sunday. They brought with them the letters from Josette and a small treat for the children. They always had Mother preview the letters before they gave them to the children to make sure there was nothing in them that may be upsetting. Their next visit was going to be different.

The winter chill and wind arrived in Tarbes and the children were preparing for Christmas. Upon their arrival, Pierre and Lucinda were taken to Mother's office. She gave them a warm greeting. "It is so good to see you again. I hope you can stay for the Christmas concert. It will be in the chapel, and both Marcel and Nicole will be singing. Have you brought letters?"

Mother saw the tears forming in Lucinda's eyes and the sadness in Pierre's face. "Is there something wrong?" Lucinda opened her large bag and handed Mother the note they received from Viviane. "Mother, I am afraid it is tragic news for the children." Mother read the note. "Do you think this is credible?"

"Yes, we believe it is authentic and credible. Josette mentioned Viviane's name in one of her notes to us. We have also heard that the Germans are meticulous in tracking and recording the deaths of all prisoners, so perhaps at the end of this war, her name will be listed. Since she was selected to paint a portrait of the *Kommandant*, I am sure she was a notable and prominent prisoner whose death was recorded."

"Mother," said Pierre, "the death of Josette overwhelms us and I am afraid we will not be able to break this horrible news to Marcel and Nicole. We know that you have much experience telling children about the death of a parent."

"I understand, and yes, I sadly have much experience in this dialogue that always tears at my heart. It is always a difficult conversation that they will never forget. Thank you for coming, and be safe. I will tell the children that you were here."

"Thank you, Mother." Lucinda handed Mother her large bag. "Pierre and I have baked some pastries for you and the children. We wish this could be a merry Christmas, but sadly, the war continues and its atrocities impact all of us. And now another tragedy with the death of Josette."

Following the Christmas concert, Mother asked Marcel and Nicole to stay with her in the chapel. The chapel was empty as she led them to the front pew and stood in front of them as they faced the crucifix of Christ. "Children, Monsieur Pierre and Madame Lucinda were here earlier today and, as you know, they receive letters from your maman. I have some sad news that I must share with you." Marcel reached for Nicole's hand. "They received a note which said that your maman became very ill and passed away at the Auschwitz concentration camp. My heart breaks to give you this news."

Nicole gripped the pew and shouted defiantly, "No, not Maman! She promised that she would return to us. Papa was her guardian angel and he was protecting her." She looked at her brother, hoping he would tell her this wasn't true. "Marcel!"

Mother handed the note to Marcel. He read it aloud to his sister. He looked at Mother, fighting back tears of anger. "Why couldn't the Germans give her medication and make her better? Why couldn't they help her? First they kill our Papa and now Maman. When will this killing stop? When will this war be over?"

Mother sat down between them and held their hands. "I know you may never understand her death, but remember all of the good memories you have of both your maman and papa. The sorrow in your hearts may never leave and it will take time to heal your sadness. Remember the happy times the four of you shared.

"Please know that love surrounds you. It is certainly not the same love you felt from your parents, but we do love you and we will take care of you. Always be strong in your love for each other. Nicole, I know that Marcel will look after you and he will be your protector as you grow older. Time will help to ease the sorrow and anger you are feeling now. You will never forget the love your parents gave you."

Nicole pointed at the crucifix. "Why did Jesus let this happen?" she asked through her tears. "I thought he would protect Maman and bring her back to us."

How many times Mother had been asked that question, and how many times she had struggled to respond with an adequate answer. She had been witness to so much loss, so much despair, so much evil. So she let Nicole's question hang there, heavy, between them, in the space between faith and doubt.

The months passed, and usually, when the weather allowed, Marcel and Nicole continued their Saturday morning meetings. Marcel told Nicole that he met some new boys and made new friends. He told her about Raphael. He and Raphael slept next to each other and were becoming fast friends. Once a week following dinner, they cleaned the pots and dishes. They both were altar boys. They played soccer with the other boys, and Marcel discovered that Raphael played the trumpet which he kept under his bed. Raphael told him about the death of his parents in the train bombing and that his father was a famous singer and trumpet player.

Following Mother's conversation with them concerning the death of their mother, Marcel noticed a change in Nicole's behavior. She was quiet and expressed little interest in anything that Marcel told her. She had a vacant stare and nothing seemed important. Their conversations had been one-sided, brief, and usually ended with Nicole crying. Marcel understood her feelings and her depression, as he, too, was having a difficult time accepting the loss of both of his parents at the hands of the Germans. His new life here at the orphanage would never replace the life and love he once had in Lourdes. He had a hard time accepting the message that Mother and the other staff continued to repeat: "Don't look back; look ahead."

The next Saturday when they met, Marcel saw a change in Nicole's attitude and her emotions seemed to be more under control. She gave him a warm kiss and told him how much she loved him. She also told Marcel how much she disliked her studies and her teacher, Sister Agatha. "What I do like, Marcel, is helping the little girls learn to read. I read books to them. My dormitory Sister also lets me help her wash and dress the little ones in the morning. I like when they keep me busy." Her tone became more serious.

"Yesterday Mother came to visit with me. She said that a family is coming tomorrow afternoon and they want to meet me. What if they will like me and want to adopt me? I don't want to be adopted because then I would leave you here and I would miss you."

Marcel gave her a kiss and smiled encouragingly. "If you can, bring them over to see me. I would love to meet them. Nicole, if they are a loving family, you can start a new life with them. Whatever happens, don't be worried about me. We will always be brother and sister and we will always be together in our hearts."

On Sunday afternoon, Sister Aubree was asked to bring Nicole to meet with Mother. Sister Aubree and Nicole entered Mother's office to find her sitting with a young couple in front of her desk full of papers. Sister Aubree pulled up a chair and placed it next to Mother, who motioned to Nicole to sit next to her. Sister Aubree kissed Nicole on the cheek and hurried out.

Mother reached for Nicole's hand. "Nicole, this is Monsieur Maxime and Madame Justine Colbert. I have told them all about you and your brother and the tragic deaths of your maman and papa. The Colberts would like to adopt a child, Nicole. They have no children. They live on a small farm near Ibos with horses, chickens, and a dog named Sadie. They wanted to meet you, and I told them you would walk with them and show them around our campus. Please try to find Marcel so they can meet him, too. Take as much time as you like, but remember, dinner is at six."

Maxime and Justine held Nicole's hands as she walked them over to meet Marcel, who was on the soccer field with Raphael. He saw Nicole walking toward him and waved to her. He introduced himself to the Colberts, and Nicole excitedly told him that they had a farm in Ibos with animals. Marcel told them about their bakery in Lourdes and how he helped make deliveries. "I really enjoyed making deliveries to the Catholic Church in Ibos. I think it was called St. Marks."

Justine told him that they are Catholic and that was the church they attend. They talked awhile longer, and then Nicole rushed the couple off toward her dormitory where she introduced them to some of the girls and showed them her room. The afternoon flew by. They made their way back to Mother's office. She looked up from her cluttered desk. "Well, how was your visit?" Maxime was still holding Nicole's hand.

"Mother, she did an outstanding job. What a beautiful campus! She took us to the chapel where we said a prayer. We so enjoyed our time with her."

Mother handed Justine a folder full of papers. "These are the legal papers for your consideration. Did Nicole tell you that she loves to read to our little ones and helps keep them neat and clean? She is also an excellent student!"

Sister Aubree appeared at the door. Mother stood to say adieu. "Thank you for meeting Nicole and visiting with us today. Think about your time with her, and if you care to return next Sunday for another visit, please contact me." Sister Aubree took Nicole by the hand. Maxime and Justine each gave her a kiss. "Thank you Nicole. It's been a wonderful afternoon. We will see you soon." Nicole waved goodbye as Sister Aubree walked her back to her dormitory.

"I think we have fallen in love with her, Mother. Can we come back next Sunday and take her with us? Maxime and I know that she will complete our family. This has been a very special day!"

"Nicole is a beautiful child and I know you will be loving parents. I will need some time to check your references and complete my official forms. I will have her birth and baptismal certificates for you. I have been attempting to expedite child placement, especially in light of the German occupation. I never know when the German soldiers will stop here and demand to search our buildings. Would you please come back in a fortnight? That should give me enough time to work through my checklist and allow you a bit more time for discernment. It will also help Nicole to settle her emotions, especially since she will be leaving her brother."

Justine and Maxime shook Mother's hand. "That will be fine. It also gives us time to ready the house and prepare her bedroom."

Mother showed them out and then walked over to Nicole's dormitory. She found her sitting on her bed reading a book to one of the younger girls. "Nicole, you are a busy girl today. I must speak with you. Excuse us, Kathleen. We will not be long before you can continue your book." Mother walked Nicole to a small sofa located near the front entrance.

"Nicole, I have some exciting news for you. Monsieur Maxime and Madam Justine want you to come and live with them. They so enjoyed meeting you today and can't wait to take you to their home. They would like to adopt you. You will start a new life with them. In just two weeks, you will be in your new home. Does this news make you happy?"

Nicole was apprehensive. "It does make me happy, but it also makes me sad. I will have to leave Marcel. I will miss him." Mother reached for her hand.

"Marcel will always be your brother and you can visit him here. He will always be a part of your life wherever you are. He will be happy for you. Go find him now and tell him the good news. Then you both can come to the evening meal."

As word spread quickly among Nicole's friends and classmates, Nicole's apprehension turned into excitement. On her last Sunday morning at St. Stephen's, she attended Mass with Marcel. After the service he walked her to her dormitory and helped her pack her meager belongings. They both walked over to Mother's office and awaited the arrival of the Colberts.

Justine and Maxime arrived promptly at 10:00 in their old pick-up truck and helped Nicole place her two small bags behind the front seat. Marcel and Nicole cried and hugged and kissed adieu. Maxime shook Marcel's hand.

"Marcel, Justine and I want you to know that you are welcome to come visit your sister. Please don't become a stranger. Mother told us that Sunday visits are permissible."

"Thank you, Monsieur. I look forward to visiting my sister in her new home."

As they pulled away, Nicole leaned out the window and cried, "I love you Marcel! Please come to see me!"

Marcel waved back, his heart swelling with love, pride, and hope for his sister. But all he could think was *another goodbye.*

Twenty
March, 1944

The Arrest of Mother Anne Marie

One Friday morning the children at the Orphanage of St. Stephen were busy in their classrooms when the chapel bells and the sirens began to sound. The children and their instructors knew what to do. If they heard the chapel bells first and then the sirens, they knew that the Germans had arrived and that they had to exit the buildings and wait in the courtyard. Marcel walked out of his classroom with Raphael next to him—two thirteen-year-old boys in the ninth grade, nervous and afraid. This was the second time the Germans had arrived to search the campus since the beginning of the year. The boys knew the Germans might take hours to complete their work, so they began the long wait on this very chilly but sunny March morning.

Today felt different to Marcel as he eyed the large contingent of soldiers with their trucks and military vehicles parked in front of the chapel. He remembered conversations he overheard between his father and mother regarding secret hiding places within the orphanage where Mother would hold Jewish children and downed airmen until they could be taken by passeurs across the mountains to Spain.

Marcel saw one of the trucks pull around and park behind the convent. He watched as two boys in school uniforms with their hands tied behind their backs were being pushed down the convent steps along with two men dressed in camouflage. Mother Anne Marie, dressed in her black habit with a black scarf wrapped around her head instead of her white cornette, walked in front of a soldier with his rifle pointed at her back, her face grim. A second truck pulled in, and two German soldiers carried a large file cabinet down the steps and placed it in the back. They then unfurled a large cloth sign and hung it over the convent door: *Death to Collaborators*.

Raphael was terrified. "Marcel, they are arresting Mother! Do you think she was hiding the other four? And the sign, Marcel. What is going to happen to her?" The nuns from the convent ran toward Mother, pleading with the soldiers to release her.

Marcel tried to stay steady and calm. "I am afraid for her, Raphael, for what the Germans are going to do. She only wanted to help Jewish children escape this Nazi terror, and for that she is going to be punished." The trucks and cars pulled out of the orphanage and headed toward Tarbes.

Sister Aubree walked toward the gathering of staff and children waiting in the courtyard. Her voice was loud and strong. "Because of the German raid this morning and the arrest of Mother Anne Marie, we will have early dismissal. Please study in your dormitory rooms until the evening meal is served. All of the older boys in grade nine, please come with me for clean-up duty."

Marcel and Raphael, along with three other boys, followed Sister Aubree to the convent. Sister Aubree took a deep breath as she faced the realization of assuming Mother's leadership role. She took the boys to Mother's office and was horrified to see the destruction. There were files and papers everywhere, furniture overturned, windows broken. She turned to the boys. "We need to find some trash containers for this mess." They went down the narrow stairs and into the basement. Sister knew the rooms that Mother used to hide her "angels." She entered each room and saw clothes, shoes, and blankets thrown about. She found a large empty cardboard box and handed it to Marcel.

"Here, take this to the office. They can place the papers in here but no broken glass. I'll find a container for that." Marcel hurried upstairs as Sister picked up a large metal container standing next to the furnace. As she closed the door, she saw a shadow moving toward her. She froze in fear. As it came closer, the shadow transformed into a tall male figure dressed in a tan uniform. A quiet voice spoke to her in excellent French. Sister Aubree held tightly to the metal container.

"Sister, don't be frightened. I am one of the 'angels' those German soldiers didn't find. I am not an Allied airman but a French prisoner of war who was able to escape our detainment camp near Lyon. My name is Jules. I wanted to join the Resistance here in this area and was told to see Mother Anne Marie. Mother said I could stay hidden until a Resistance fighter came to show me the way to their camp. As soon as I heard the bells and sirens, I hid in the coal bin. Thank God they did not find me. I heard the yelling and commotion so I assume the others were found and taken. Is Mother safe?"

Sister relaxed her stance. "No, she was taken away along with the two Jewish boys and two Allied airmen. I fear for her safety. The Germans show no mercy. As you know, they will not hesitate to murder the innocent, even our nuns, priests, and brothers. No one is protected from their brutality. I must find a new place for you to hide. They may return at any time."

On Wednesday evening of the week following the German raid and arrest of Mother Anne Marie, Sister Aubree had just returned from evening prayers to Mother's office when she heard a soft knock on the convent door. She pulled back the room-darkening shades and looked out the window. Turning on the porch light, she saw a black man dressed in dark clothes with a beret pulled down over his eyes. She recalled Mother speaking of a black man who had helped her obtain forged documents from the Abbey of St. Anthony. She held her breath and opened the door as Diop stepped forward and extended his hand.

"Bon soir. I am Diop, a member of the Resistance and a friend of Mother Anne Marie. Our contact here has told us about the German raid and the arrest of Mother. You must be Sister Aubree. I was told you have someone hiding here who needs to be moved to our camp. Is that correct?"

"Yes, I am Sister Aubree. Mother did mention your name to me and told me about your activities. I have a Resistance member hiding here and he wants to join your camp. Please have a seat. I will go get him." Sister left the office and returned in a few minutes with Jules in tow carrying his rucksack. Diop and Jules exchanged the secret code words of their Resistance groups and then shook hands.

"Diop," said Sister, "I have something to discuss with you concerning one of our children staying here whom you may know. His name is Marcel. Both of his parents have died at the hands of the Germans. Marcel and his sister Nicole arrived here last summer. His sister was recently adopted, but Marcel is still with us."

"Yes, Sister, I know them well. I was the one who brought them here in September last. I worked for their parents at the bakery in Lourdes. I knew their papa was murdered and their maman was taken to Drancy by the SS, but I did not know that their maman had died or that Nicole had been adopted."

"I am very concerned about Marcel. The Germans now know that we have been hiding Jewish children here. During their raid they took many of our secret files. My fear is that they will return to match a child to their records. If they find a child whose record shows a Jewish parent, that child will be arrested. As you know, many of our Jewish children have been taken by passeurs over the Pyrénées to Spain and then to Portugal and England. Claude, Marcel's father, was one of those passeurs. Marcel is in danger, Diop. Do you think you could take Marcel with you and help him escape from France?"

"Sister, I am not in a position to take Marcel to my camp until I receive permission from my commander. I can tell you that we have a series of safe houses and trained guides who have taken airmen and Jewish children from France across the Pyrénées to a safe haven in Spain. I have accompanied one of the guides on several of these walks, which as you can imagine are very dangerous. So there is danger here, but also danger crossing the Pyrénées. I do understand your concern. Let me take Jules to our camp and I will return with news as soon as possible."

Just over a week later, on a Sunday afternoon, Diop returned to the orphanage and found the back door that Sister Aubree told him to use. He knocked three times. A young sister opened the door and asked him to come in. "Please remain here while I find Sister. She alerted us that you may be visiting."

Sister Aubree walked up the long corridor with Marcel by her side. Marcel ran toward Diop and gave him a warm embrace. They followed Sister into the office and sat at a round wooden table.

"Diop, I hope you don't mind that I invited Marcel. He and I have had an honest discussion about my concerns and the danger for him if he stays here at the orphanage. He understands that there may be a possibility that you can arrange passage for him to Spain, with England as a final destination. As you can see, he is getting taller and is now thirteen years old. I told him that most adoptions from here usually occur more frequently for children under twelve years of age."

"You have grown since the last time that I saw you, Marcel! Such a handsome young man! I was surprised and happy to hear that Nicole was adopted, but I know you miss her. I did discuss your situation with our resistance commander, Colonel Emile Dumond. Due to the recent raids here, the Colonel has created a new starting point for what we have been calling our "Freedom Passage." Our Resistance network throughout southern France has been informed that downed pilots and civilians will no longer come to this orphanage for passage across the Pyrénées Mountains. Usually our Resistance camp does two passages a month into Spain, and the Colonel tells me we now have two airmen waiting to make the trek. He would not guarantee you passage until he has a chance to meet you. Marcel, it is a very dangerous hike over the mountains, but I am certain you could do it. What are your feelings?"

Marcel was contemplative, trying to visualize his future. He understood that life was all about possibilities. He looked intently at Sister Aubree and Diop.

"What I am hearing you and Sister say is that I am not safe living here at the orphanage because my maman was Jewish and I need to move on. I have been reading about world history and the United States of America. We have had discussions about America in our classes. My friend Raphael, his father was a soldier from the United States who stayed in France after the Great War. His father told him many stories of life in America.

"When you take soldiers and others across the mountains, what is their final destination? Can I travel to America? Will I live in an orphanage in Spain? I am confused and afraid, and I want you to tell me what to do. I am alone. My parents are gone and my sister has found a new life. No one knows how much longer this war will continue, and the longer it continues the more danger comes to all of us."

Diop glanced at Sister Aubree and then touched Marcel's arm. "Marcel, I know your world has been devastated, but you must remain strong. We do have your future on our minds and want to do what is best for you. When we take French children to Spain, many will stay until the end of the war and then most likely make their way back to France. Others may travel to England and then to America or Canada. I have heard that several children are now with foster families in England, and some are in the United States. America is a land of opportunity and promise. Just remember what Mother Anne Marie would say: 'Life is a series of new beginnings!'"

Marcel turned Diop's words over in his mind. "Diop, I trust you and know that you want me to be safe and someday find happiness. I have no idea where my life is going. Let me get my rucksack and say adieu to my friends. I am ready for a new beginning."

Twenty One
March, 1944

Marcel Walks the
Pyrénées Mountains

Diop continued to use the old bakery truck as he and Marcel drove from the orphanage in Tarbes to the forested area near Gan, France, almost eight kilometers from Pau. Diop took some back roads that bypassed Pau due to the German presence at the airfield and possible road blocks. Marcel was talkative as they drove on this late Sunday evening. Diop told him that the ride would be about two hours to the new camp recently established by the Resistance near the Pyrénées foothills. "I will hide the truck in the heavily-wooded area and then we'll walk for about an hour. We should arrive at the camp just before darkness sets in."

Marcel provided Diop with more information about the death of his maman at Aushwitz and about Nichole's adoption. He was also curious about the activities of the Resistance. "So what have you been doing to these Germans? How many have you killed?" Diop told Marcel in limited detail what he had been tasked to do by Colonel Emile Dumond. He described his trips to visit the friars who forged documents for Mother Anne Marie, and the attacks on the German troop trains and the Pau airfield.

"Marcel, the airfield attack was my most horrifying experience. Our friend René was killed in that attack, and I was wounded in the shoulder. I was so close to being killed. That experience taught me what war is all about. Every day I pray to God to keep me safe. When I was your age, I never imagined that I would be killing German soldiers. Marcel, I was saddened to hear about the murder of your papa and the death of your maman. As you know, I was close to them and considered them family. It seems that death totally surrounds us. I want to do what I can to move you to a safe haven."

Diop slowed the truck and turned off the empty road onto a crushed stone trail. Large pine trees enveloped them. Diop moved the truck into the thick underbrush and covered it with a camouflage tarp that he took from behind the front seat. Marcel found his rucksack and the two began their walk through the forest along mountain streams and into the gradually sloping foothills as the sun began to set. Diop had taken this particular trail only one other time and repeatedly checked his compass for the camp's map coordinates. Marcel tripped several times on the slippery terrain and cut his head on a low-hanging sharp tree branch.

After almost an hour of strained concentration through rough terrain, they were met by a Resistance fighter who emerged from behind a large granite boulder with rifle in hand. Diop recognized him. It was José. He lowered his rifle and walked toward them. Diop told Marcel that he liked José and was impressed with his language skills, speaking Spanish, French, and English. Diop introduced José to Marcel and gave him information about the deaths of Marcel's parents, his sister's adoption, their bakery, and the orphanage.

As they headed into camp, Marcel smelled smoke and detected the essence of grilled meat. A large campfire was warming the chill of the cold March evening. As Diop and Marcel walked toward the fire, a large group of fighters surrounded them. Soon Colonel Dumond appeared. "Diop, this must be the young man you told me about. Welcome!" Marcel shook his hand.

"Colonel, thank you for allowing me to come to your camp and for helping me escape."

"You are very welcome. I am anxious to speak with you. In the meantime, let me introduce you to Leo Brevard." A tall young man with blond hair extended his hand to Marcel. "Leo recently joined us as well. You two will be tent mates for a brief time until we firm up a travel plan.

"You must be hungry, Marcel. Have something to eat while Leo introduces you to some of our fighters. It should be a quiet night. Tomorrow morning you and I will talk. I'm glad you are with us."

Marcel ate some goat stew with vegetables from the big stew pot hanging over the fire. After brief introductions and light conversation with some of the fighters, Marcel followed Leo to their tent. Leo handed Marcel some wool blankets and a sweater. "Hopefully you won't be too cold. You need to layer your clothes. Here, try these socks and gloves. The camp has a large wooden bin full of clothes of all sizes where you can find a good pair of boots. If we will be hiking in the mountains together, we should take the warmest clothes we can find. I've been told this has been a particularly snowy winter."

They settled in, turned off the lamp, and talked quietly in the dark. Leo told Marcel about his life. He was fifteen when he made his way to Toulouse from Nice. His parents were both doctors at the hospital in Nice. The Germans raided their home and arrested his parents, who were Jewish. Leo escaped and hid in a crawl space under their house. When he felt it was safe, he went to his aunt and uncle's house which was nearby. They, too, were in danger and afraid of arrest. They left Nice and drove to Toulouse to hide with a friend who was a member of the Resistance. A decision was made for Leo to escape via the Freedom Passage. "So here I am, waiting to walk the mountain trail to Spain. My hope is that I will eventually return to France and be re-united with my parents when the war is over. These are frightening times, Marcel."

Marcel lay on the cold, damp ground with two blankets as his mattress and two as covers. He told Leo about his family and the loss of his parents. "Leo, there is hope for you that you will see your parents again. I have no hope for that. My only family is my sister, and it may be a very long time before I see her again. I have no idea where my life is heading. I can only pray and hope. I live day to day." He paused.

"Tomorrow brings our future, Leo, so let's get some sleep." Marcel made the sign of the cross, said a quick prayer, and pulled the blankets closer to his chin.

The cold morning brought little sun with mostly clouds moving above the dense pine forest. Diop found Leo and Marcel standing near the fire eating some tepid oat broth from tin cups. "Good morning. I hope you slept well. Colonel Dumond would like to talk to both of you."

They walked over to the colonel's tent and found him seated at a small wooden table with José and two men in tattered uniforms and military coats standing in front of him. "Bonjour, mes amis." The colonel spoke in French to the boys; José translated in English for the airmen. "I will be as brief as possible. The four of you are the team that will trek the Pyrénées together. We have two American airmen, Tim Kelly and Mark

Webb; and two boys, Marcel and Leo, who are French. They are evading the Germans because they are of Jewish descent.

"I believe everyone has met José. He is Basque Spanish and he will be your guide. Tomorrow morning he will start the four of you on your journey to San Sebastian, Spain. He will stay with you until you reach the British Consulate. Besides being a good fighter, he is an excellent mountain guide and knows the trail well. He also has handpicked the safe houses where you will stay.

"This afternoon I will give you forged identity cards along with transit and exit visas. The boys will also receive baptismal certificates. José will give each of you a walking stick, a goatskin bag for your water, and hopefully he will find each of you a pair of espadrille boots. You already have your rucksacks. Take some bread and whatever else you can find that will satisfy your hunger. Food will be scarce.

"Depending on how much snow is still on the slopes and the weather, your trek may take five or six days, but perhaps a bit longer if you encounter German or Spanish border squads. You will walk primarily at night, so let's pray for a bright moon. Are there any questions?" The four looked at each other, then shook their heads.

"Very well, then." The colonel stood and shook their hands. "I wish each of you a safe trip. May God be with you! You are now in the hands of José. Diop, a word." The others filed out of the tent.

"I just received a message that they will be closing the orphanage. We may have some children coming to our camp until we can locate a safe haven for them and the remaining staff. Some of the children may be housed in the Catholic Church at Tarbes. I need you to begin working out the logistics with Sister Aubree."

Diop looked for Marcel and found him organizing his sack and clothing. "Marcel, I just left the colonel. He told me that a decision has been made to close the orphanage. Thank God you left when you did and that your sister was adopted."

"Oh, Diop, will you be able to help the children remaining there? Can you please help Raphael? He is a good soccer player, and you would be a great coach. Please watch over him!"

"I will do my best, Marcel. But you must concentrate on your journey tomorrow. Please be careful. It will be dangerous. Who knows when we will meet again? Just remember that I love you and will be forever thankful for the love of your family."

"I have no idea where I will land, Diop, but hopefully someday we can reunite. How many lives will this war tear apart? Please be safe and don't take chances. And if you can, please keep in touch with Nicole. Sister Aubree has the name and address of the family that adopted her. She would love to see you. Tell her that someday I will see her again. I miss her so much."

"Marcel, with both of us not knowing where we will be in the future when peace returns, I am trying to think of a connection that will help us find each other. The Rosary Basilica is the church we attended in Lourdes. I am thinking that at some point I will make my way back there and connect with the priest. I will give him my information and tell him that if he ever receives any mail addressed to me, to hold it.

"After the war I would like to return to Lourdes and open a boulangerie just like the one your parents had. Maybe we can be partners? We know about miracles; we know they can happen. You will write me in care of the Basilica and tell me where you are living and give me an address. Does that sound like a plan?"

Marcel nodded his head. "When I find a place to live, I will send a letter to the Basilica. I am hopeful that we will see each other again. You will be my connector. I am going to miss you, Diop. I hope we can reunite!"

Marcel found his wallet with his identity papers stuffed in the bottom of his sack. He pulled out a tattered picture of his maman and papa standing in the garden behind the bakery, holding hands. He showed it to Diop. "I look at this photograph every night after I say my prayers. I ask them to protect Nicole and me, and now I will ask them to protect you as well. We are family."

Twenty Two
March, 1944

Danger on the Mountain Trail

It was a sun-filled morning and the mountain air brought a cold chill to Marcel's face. Leo and he rummaged through the clothes bin and were lucky to find some warm hiking clothes even though the fit was not perfect. They were dressed in long underwear, sweaters, hooded rain jackets, and bulky snow pants, and each was wearing two pairs of wool socks. They hoped their boots were waterproof and their gloves would protect their hands from the freezing cold, snow, and ice. José told them that the temperatures at night would be below zero at the higher elevations. The two airmen were bundled but not layered, and Tim could not find a pair of hiking boots that fit. All four wore knit hats that hardly covered their ears.

José gathered the group and told them that this route was the safest, with very few German and Spanish patrols and checkpoints. He handed each a hiking stick and a folded piece of paper which contained a crude map of their trek over the Pyrénées from Gan, France to San Sebastián, Spain. He pointed to Leruns, which he told them was their destination for today, and that they would be walking mainly through pine forests and back trails. The trek today would be in daylight, which would be the exception. José was carrying his rifle and hunting knife. His rucksack, at fifty pounds or more, was strapped tightly to his back. He pointed ahead with his compass in hand.

With José in the lead, they started out in single file: Tim, Mark, Leo, and lastly Marcel. José told them to try to maintain six feet of distance between them and to walk in silence. "Keep your eyes on me, and if I see anything suspicious, I will motion you to kneel or crawl, so follow my gestures. This section of the trail is safe, but if you notice anything, tap the one in front of you. Today we will walk over twenty miles. Enjoy the view. After today, most of our trek will be at night."

The group walked along a stone path through sun-dappled woods and then began a long ascent along granite boulders and waterfalls. Marcel was hoping to see some wildlife. His father told him stories of black bears, red deer, and mountain goats on his journeys through the mountains. Marcel knew he must stay focused on the trail beneath him—tripping meant falling and falling meant danger—but he would appreciate the distraction of the wildlife. As the hours passed, they left the lowlands behind them and move past the tree line.

José finally allowed them to stop to eat lunch next to a small pond with a bubbling spring. After they filled their water pouches from the spring, they sat on a large boulder, elbow to elbow, grateful for the rest and food. Tim untied his boots.

"My feet are hurting already. These boots are too tight." Mark looked over at Leo and Marcel.

"So give Tim and me some background about the two of you." He looked at José to translate. Leo spoke first and told them about his parents, their arrest, and his escape from Nice.

Marcel then told them his brief tragic story. Marcel looked at José. "Ask them why the Germans hate the Jews."

"When the Allies arrest Hitler, they will ask him that question," answered Tim. "That is one of the reasons Mark and I joined the US Air Force—to help win this war and defeat this Nazi terror. We both want to return to England and fly again. We hear that a large invasion is soon to happen, and our revenge will be swift. You boys have been through so much trauma in your young lives. We admire your courage."

José translated as Tim and Mark shared their stories. Tim was married and from Charlotte, North Carolina. Mark was single and lived with his parents in Ft. Collins, Colorado, prior to enlisting. They recounted the story of the downing of their aircraft over northern France. These brief introductions served their purpose: The four were friends now, not strangers, all connected in this world war.

The afternoon hike continued and the sun began to set behind the mountains. They walked through a deciduous forest and saw goats and sheep grazing in a mountain pasture. José led them toward a clearing where they saw acres of mostly sloping open space. In the distance was a small shepherd's cottage sitting under several large, moss-draped firs. José pointed ahead. "This is where we will spend the night. Stay here behind these trees while I check to be sure the house is empty."

José made his way back. "This cottage belongs to my friend who lives not far from here. It is empty and will be warm once we find some firewood." As they walked toward the cottage, they saw the glittering lights from the town of Leruns in the distance. José, Marcel, and Leo dropped their shoulder sacks at the door and headed into the forest to gather firewood.

Mark and Tim opened the cottage door to find a large room with exposed log beams and a small fireplace. "So far a good day," remarked Tim. "I thought the boys would slow us down, but they are in good shape and seem excited to be on this journey. José said that the route we are taking is one of the safest. I think that tomorrow we enter Spain. Wonder if we will see any German patrols at the border?"

"I heard that the Wehrmacht were moving their forces closer to Normandy in anticipation of an Allied invasion. So maybe we will be lucky."

José and the boys appeared in the doorway, Marcel and Leo carrying firewood and José holding up two dead rabbits. "José found us dinner!" Leo exclaimed.

"The passeurs always set traps behind the cottage," said José. "I'll take these outside and butcher them while you fellows get a hot fire started."

The sun began to set and the fireplace lit the room. The rabbit dinner was meager for five people, so they shared some leftovers from their sacks. José wiped his mouth on his sleeve, left for a moment, and returned with a sack of dried apples.

"Here, divide these up. This is tomorrow's food. Our next meal will be much better. The safe house in Jaca, Spain, never disappoints. We will stay with an older couple who own a very popular restaurant there." He smiled. "They happen to be my aunt and uncle. I was born in Jaca; my parents moved to Galar, but I still have family there. The Aragón River runs near Jaca, but we will not cross it until we come to the town of Sangüesa. They have Spanish border patrols near there.

"Also, Jaca is about 3,000 feet above sea level. Occasionally someone may feel sick due to the altitude, causing headaches, vomiting, and sometimes dizziness. Let me know if you are not feeling well. I carry some medicine that may help. Tomorrow will be a long day. Sleep late. We will head out tomorrow afternoon and walk the rest of the day and then all night. The distance from Leruns to Jaca is about fifty miles. The trails will be difficult, snow-covered, and icy as we move higher. This will be the most dangerous part of our hike."

The next day brought gusty winds and sleet with plunging temperatures. José took them on a winding stone trail that moved higher along the side of a large, snow-covered mountain. Marcel's face was burning as the wind increased. The temperature continued to drop and Marcel was frantic to find one of his gloves. He thought he might have dropped it at the cottage. His maman always told him how forgetful he was. He tried to force his hand into the much-too-small pocket of his coat, but the pressure on his sore fingers was painful. He had to keep pace with the group and not worry about his hand.

Six hours into their trek the sun began to set. José found a small cave that he used on past trips. The five were exhausted as they fell on the rocky floor. All were hurting with wind burn, bleeding blisters, and sore backs and legs. They took off their boots and rubbed their aching feet. Marcel told them that he lost the glove for his left hand. José looked through his rucksack. "Sorry, Marcel, but I did not bring any extra gloves. Try to keep your hand inside your coat. Frostbite can happen quickly."

José untied a thick rope that had been attached to his sack. "This will be a short rest, so I need to explain how we will use this rope. As the night surrounds us, you will be walking blind. This rope will help keep us connected. Each of you will loop this around your right hand. The rope connects you to the person ahead of you. My rule of silence will be broken when we encounter a hazard or some other obstacle that may present danger. If the rope slackens, we stop. Tonight we walk up the mountain; as day breaks, we walk down. The good news is that, on the morrow, we will be close to our safe house for food and rest."

They moved out of the cave into the all-embracing darkness, holding on to the rope now looped around their right hands. The sleet turned to snow and the falling temperature continued to tear at their lungs. Marcel was told to take short breaths after he described feeling like he had fire in his chest. He could barely feel his feet, and several of his fingers on his bare hand were numb. The hours passed and José offered no respite. The group of five began to take baby steps as the trail became a more slippery, snow-covered, steep ascent.

Suddenly Leo lost his footing and fell against an outcrop of limestone. In the darkness, Marcel fell on top of him. Both boys screamed as they slid closer to the ledge. Sure death was less than two feet away. Leo grasped for something to cling to. He flailed his arms and found a juniper limb, holding on to it tightly as Marcel slid hard against his leg.

José told Tim and Mark to take a knee as he dropped the rope and went back to find the boys. He followed the rope line and could see their faint shadows. He moved in the direction of their voices. Marcel was crawling toward José, pulling Leo by the hand. José helped Marcel to his feet and knelt in front of Leo.

"Leo, can you stand? Where is your pain?" Marcel and José assisted him as blood streamed down his face. "What really hurts is a gash over my left eye." José removed his scarf from around his neck, wrapped it around Leo's head, and tied it tightly. "Are you sure that is all that hurts? The scarf will help to stop the bleeding."

José felt the limestone outcrop. He told Mark and Tim to move toward the two boys and him and to sit close to each other. "Time to take a break. We almost lost you two." José took his first aid kit and torch light from his rucksack. "I hesitate to turn on the torch, but since we are under cover, I think it will not be seen. I need some light to see this gash."

José handed the torch to Marcel who held it close as José cleaned the wound and fastened a bandage with tape and gauze. "Leo, you lost a little blood, but you will heal. This should hold until we reach San Sebastián. There you can have a doctor take a look. It may require stitches."

José saw that the four were shaking with the cold and the aftermath of the accident. The snow continued to fall. "We will be descending now, so the worst part of this hike is hopefully behind us. Daybreak should arrive in about two hours, so that will help. We will reach Jaca by mid-morning. Stay focused and keep the faith. Good days are ahead."

Tim was skeptical. "José, this is an impossible journey, and I am losing faith. We are hurting and we can't ignore what our bodies are telling us. The freezing temperatures are unbearable. Thinking of my wife and saying my prayers are the only things sustaining me." José nodded his head.

"I never said this would be easy. We will make it. We need to stay strong."

Twenty Three
March, 1944

The Capture of Mark and Tim

The clouds cleared and the sun shone down on the mountain as the snow and ice made their way north. The mountain path widened next to a steep gully. The town of Jaca was in the distance with the river flowing close to it. The five stopped under a stand of large oaks. José raised his hand and pointed toward the town. "We are only thirty minutes away, so enjoy the morning sun. The trail crosses some streams just ahead. Follow my lead."

They crossed a wide stream and through a ravine that led them toward a whitewashed three-story Basque farmhouse replete with wooden balconies and a rust-colored terra cotta roof. Rolling green hills framed the beautiful three-story house. There was a large barn almost connected to the house with a split rail fence surrounding it. As they got closer, Marcel spied a large black bull standing near the barn. José told the group to wait at the bottom of the high steps while he announced their arrival.

José returned and told the four to follow him to the barn. They walked around several chickens and encountered the bull and two cows standing next to the entrance. Everyone fell to the barn floor in pain and exhaustion. An elderly couple came into the barn carrying blankets. José introduced them as Florentino and Ainara, his aunt and uncle. "Aunt Ainara will bring you some breakfast. Take these blankets and try to nap until the food is prepared."

Florentino set a small wooden table just inside the barn. He made several trips inside the house and brought out the breakfast Ainara prepared: goat cheese egg omelets, crusty Spanish bread, red grapes, a canister of flavored water, and several bottles of red wine. The bustle of preparation and the smell of the food awakened the four, and they couldn't believe their eyes as they rushed to the table. Ainara stood proudly by as her guests passed the food from plate to plate.

As they ate, Florentino heated large buckets of water over a fire pit. He carried the buckets of steaming water into the barn and poured cups of salt into each bucket. He motioned to José, who looked at the four as they devoured their food and pointed to the buckets. "When you are finished, take off your shoes and soak your blistering feet."

While they were soothing their feet, José looked at Marcel's frostbitten fingers. He didn't like what he saw and called Florentino over to take a look. Florentino held Marcel's hand and touched his fingers. He spoke to José in Spanish. José asked Marcel if he could feel the touching. "No, José, I have no feeling in my ring finger and my pinky finger, and why are they turning a greenish-black?"

José recognized the signs of frostbite. "Marcel, this looks very serious. You have severe frostbite and possibly gangrene. I have some salve that may help and I will wrap it. Ainara found some gloves for you. With a few more days to walk, I am worried about your hand."

José told the group that they should sleep, as they would begin the walk to Sangüesa at sunset. The four were napping as José huddled with Florentino, who told him that there were Spanish patrols on both sides of the bridge that crossed the *Río Aragón* (Aragon River) near the town. He advised José to take the alternate trail and to also avoid the wooden footbridge about two miles from the main Aragon bridge. He carefully described the location where José could find several small wooden row boats that the Resistance had hidden for river crossings by passeurs.

"Be careful there as well. The Spaniards have increased their security all along the river. If you are captured they will send all of you back to France and turn you over to the Germans." José nodded.

"I am well aware of the danger, but I was not aware of the boats. On my past treks, I would always cross the footbridge."

In mid-afternoon the group gathered with their walking sticks and rucksacks. Ainara gave each some apples and goat cheese wrapped in a brown bag. They thanked Florentino and Ainara for their kindness and hospitality.

The long trek to Sangüesa began as a full moon rose over the mountains. The travelers were still connected by the rope, even as a bright moon and cloudless sky illuminated their path. It was another cold night with temperatures well below freezing. Marcel felt the intense pain in his hand and worried about his frostbite. Thoughts were swirling in his head: *What is gangrene? When can I see a doctor? Will this trek ever end, and if and when it does, what happens to me when we reach San Sabastián?* He wondered what would come next as he fought the persistent cold and the pain that wracked his body.

In the hours they had been walking, José set a relentless pace and only stopped for fifteen minutes for them to eat and fill their water bottles. José finally slowed down and stopped at a tree-covered rocky outcrop and told them to take a pause. He explained to them that in a mile or so the trail would bend and descend toward the town of Sangüesa and the Río Aragón.

"We will cross the river in a small boat before sunrise. We must be careful. Florentino told me that the Spanish patrols have been out in numbers and have been very aggressive all along the river. Within two hours the sun will be rising, so we must hurry."

Back on the trail, the lights of the town could be seen and they heard the sounds of the river. They walked along a narrow dirt cart path that weaved along the side of the mountain but fell quickly to meet the river. They entered a dense pine forest and the river followed them. José flicked his cigarette lighter and checked his compass. The group waited quietly while he searched for the boats. Surprised to find only one small boat, he doubted that the boat would be large enough to hold all five of them. He returned, pulling the wooden row boat behind him.

José steadied the boat on the path. "Jump in. Let's see if it will hold us. Tim, you and Mark will row. The boys will sit in the rear and I'll sit on the front seat. It will be tight but I think we can make it."

Tim stumbled into the boat, followed by Marcel and Leo. Mark could already see that it was too crowded. "José, there is no way all five of us will fit in this boat. You will have to make two trips." José agreed. "We will make two crossings. I will take the boys over first, then return for both of you."

José guided the boat into the tranquil water. Leo sat up front and Marcel was in the rear. José took the oars. "It is a clear night so I should be able to easily see you when I come back." As José rowed, he told the boys that when they reached the other side, to hide behind some trees and wait there for his return with Tim and Mark.

"When you see my lighter flicker that will be your signal to move toward the boat. I will not be long, maybe fifteen minutes. Keep a keen eye."

The boat scraped the bottom and the boys jumped out and headed for the trees. José deftly maneuvered the boat back across the river in the direction of the airmen. About halfway over he saw what looked like a large truck with a searchlight moving slowly along the river bank in the location where Tim and Mark were waiting. José prayed that the Spanish Guardia would not find them, but his prayers went unanswered. Silhouettes of soldiers with rifles pointed and dogs tethered moved along the river bank like apparitions. He could only surmise by the sharp staccato barking of the dogs that the airmen had been captured by the Spanish patrol.

He turned the boat around and rowed back to where he dropped off the boys. As the boat bumped the river bank he flicked his lighter. The boys moved down the rocky sides of the river bank and found José pulling the boat out of the water alone. "Where are Mark and Tim?" José avoided their eyes as he searched for fern bracken to hide the boat. Brusquely he responded.

"They were captured by the Spanish patrol. There was nothing I could do to save them."

"What happened, José?" Marcel asked gently. Although angry and upset, José knew the boys deserved an explanation.

"It was a helpless situation. Halfway across the river, I saw them in the spotlight. Then I saw the soldiers and heard the dogs. It was too late. If only this boat were larger, this would not have happened! I don't think the Spanish Guardia saw me, but we need to move quickly to our next safe house. Now, it is just the three of us."

José searched for the trail now that they were on the other side of the Río Aragón and found it just as the sun was rising over Sangüesa. They hiked the steep descent of the Monte Peña trail that led them to the rear of the Convent of Saint Francis of Assisi on the outskirts of town. José found a stand of trees and shrubs and told the boys to hide there until he returned. "I will not be long. The convent sisters are expecting us. We will stay here until late afternoon and then move on."

José knocked in code on the old wooden door: four taps, pause, three taps, pause, and then two final taps. One of the Franciscan nuns opened the heavy door. She remembered José from previous visits with airmen and Jewish children. José stepped inside the arched doorway. "I have two young boys with me," he said, and pointed toward the mountain trail.

"We were notified of your forthcoming arrival. All is safe and well here. Please bring them in. I am Sister Regina." José fetched the boys, and Sister Regina led them all into the kitchen area and seated them on a bench next to a long table. The Mother Superior entered the room.

"José, did all go well? I was told you were also bringing two airmen?" Sister Regina served hot coffee as José described the events of their journey to Mother Superior in Spanish.

José looked at Marcel. "I just explained to Mother the situation with Tim and Mark and asked her if someone could look at your fingers. Also, you boys take off your espadrilles and rest your feet. Mother said she will find some dry, warm socks for you."

Sister Regina prepared hot oatmeal and sausage. The boys thought nothing so simple had ever tasted so good. They thanked her and went to sit by the roaring fireplace in the rear of the kitchen. After a few minutes, Sister Regina sat down next to them with a large tin box full of medical supplies.

She saw that Marcel had not removed the glove on his left hand. Sister spoke some French and asked him to remove his glove. She had seen gangrene many times over the years and knew that Marcel's fingers were badly infected. There was a reddish line on both of his swollen fingers turning black around the affected tissue. Marcel told her that his fingers were numb and they had no feeling. Sister looked through her supplies and found some salve and Epsom salt. She warmed some water and poured it into a cup with some salt. Sister told him to soak his hand for a while, and then she would apply the cream and wrap it. She handed him four pills and a glass of water. "Take two now and save two for later. The pills will help with your pain."

Just before noon, Sister Regina led the three to a spacious, empty closet behind a small chapel. She placed blankets and pillows on the floor. José told the boys that they would sleep now and then continue their trek to Pamplona, a distance of thirty miles. José lay down next to the boys. Leo asked José how much further until they reached San Sebastián.

"This will be our last night in the mountains. On this path the maximum elevation is just over two thousand feet, so not as bad as you experienced before. There shouldn't be that much snow and ice, so we will not be bound by the rope. When we reach Pamplona, the passeurs at the safe house there can hide us in a vehicle and take us to the British Consulate in San Sebastián. I am so proud of both of you. You are brave, strong, and resilient. Your destination is close."

Twenty Four
March, 1944

Frostbite and Gangrene

Despite the reassurance from José, the mountain walk through the Pyrénées to Pamplona was still arduous, but not as physically demanding. The boys traversed soaring peaks, deep valleys, forests, streams, and rivers. Although they were enveloped in darkness they could sense the raw beauty. As they descended the mountain, the trail flattened and became easier. Pamplona snuggled against the western range of the Pyrénées and sat in a rounded valley on both sides of the Río Arga, which branched from the larger Aragón.

José found a fallen tree and told the boys that this would be their last resting stop before they reached Pamplona in about two more hours. He explained to them that they would be staying in a basement room in the Church of San Juan Bosco. "We will stay there only one night. When we reach the church our trek on foot is finished! I have made arrangements for us to travel the rest of the way to San Sabastián in a vehicle. It is a ride of about fifty miles, and much easier than walking!" The boys smiled at José, and Marcel asked, "What will happen when we reach San Sabastián and the British Consulate?"

"The British are expecting you. Our Resistance group coordinates these crossings with them. I am uncertain as to exactly what will happen to the both of you when you arrive, as there are many possibilities. There is a Consulate official who handles special situations involving children. Leo, I know you want to return to France at the end of the conflict and reunite with your parents, so they might place you in a temporary foster home. I believe there is a Jewish aid society in Spain for Jews who have fled the Germans, so they may possibly turn you over to them.

"Marcel, since both of your parents have died, you have orphan status. Please know that the British Counsel will take care of you. When we arrive in San Sabastian we need to find prompt medical care for you."

By mid-morning they arrived near the Church of San Juan Bosco. José stayed at this church on several previous trips so he knew the routine. He sat the boys on a bench on busy Estafeta Street. "Stay here while I go to the church and find Father Sergio. Do not speak with anyone. I should not be very long."

The boys sat in the beautiful warm sunshine. They were overdressed and sweating in their mountain clothing. Several people ambled by, eyeing them curiously. Leo stared at Marcel's hand, still wrapped in a heavy bandage. "How is your hand feeling?"

Marcel slowly lifted it. "I think it is getting worse. The pain is moving up my arm. Do you have some water? I want to take the two pills Sister Regina gave me, but my jug is empty." Leo found his water and handed it to Marcel.

"Thank you. The pills help a little. I had heard from my father frightening stories of people who had frostbite and gangrene. I am really worried about what might happen. I hope I can receive medical treatment soon."

"I believe the British Consul will take care of us and get you to a doctor." Leo stood and looked up and down the street, taking in the sights and sounds. "Marcel, this is a beautiful city. It reminds me of Lyon. Did you know that this is where they run the bulls every July? My father came here once with his parents when he was a boy and watched the festival. He really enjoyed it and gave me his copy of a book by a famous American author, Ernest Hemingway. It was titled *The Sun Also Rises*. You should read it. Hemingway made the Pamplona bull run famous."

Marcel looked over Leo's shoulder to see José and Father Sergio approaching. José introduced the boys to Father. "Father is going to take you to a doctor, Marcel, to have him look at your hand. I will take Leo to the church." Father spoke excellent French and told Marcel that the doctor was a friend of his. "Doctor Luis Casillas will provide good treatment for you. Are you in much pain?"

"I do have some pain and two fingers are numb. It was very cold as we were crossing the Pyrénées. I wasn't careful and lost a glove. I didn't realize how quickly frostbite could occur."

It was an easy walk to the doctor's office. After a short wait, a young receptionist took them into the office. Doctor Casillas was seated at his desk and rose to greet them. He was handsome with dark black hair, an oblong face, and goatee. Father Sergio introduced him to Marcel and provided some background about Marcel's journey. The doctor addressed him in French and took his temperature. "You do have a temperature, Marcel. I am told this frostbite occurred a few nights past as you were crossing the Pyrénées. Let me have a look at your hand."

Marcel winced as the doctor examined his fingers with his surgical probe. "You have gangrene in both fingers, caused by severe frostbite. As you can see, the gangrene has caused your fingers to turn black as a result of no blood flow. The foul-smelling brownish pus is indicative of severe infection. I am limited as to what I can do medically to improve your situation. You need hospitalization as quickly as possible." Doctor Casillas inserted a drain and removed some damaged dead skin, then applied a new bandage.

Marcel said little as he watched the doctor, but his concern was growing. "Will my fingers need to be amputated or can they be saved?"

"I will be honest with you, Marcel. Your situation is not good, and amputation is a strong possibility." The doctor looked at Father Sergio. "How long will he be here in Pamplona?"

"He is leaving tomorrow morning for San Sabastián and should be there by early afternoon. Can you secure him a placement in one of the hospitals there?"

"I know several of the staff at the Donostia University Hospital, so I will make a few telephone calls. Marcel, there is a bed in the room next to my office. You and Father can wait there while I see about making arrangements. My thought is to get you admitted as soon as you arrive in San Sabastián. Whatever plans you have may be disrupted. If we don't get you hospital care as soon as possible, you will have some major complications that may be dire. I am not trying to frighten you, but I want to be honest about your situation."

Father Sergio helped Marcel into the hospital bed. Marcel had been strong for so long, but now the tears started. "Father, Doctor Casillas said my fingers may have to be amputated. I have lost my father, my maman, my sister—and now this. I am alone, Father. I have tried to be strong, but for what? I should have stayed in France and let the Germans send me to one of their concentration camps. Please pray for me. Ask the Lord to help me find my destiny."

"Marcel, I am and will be praying for you—to stay strong and to be well. This war has tragically touched so many lives. Doctor Casillas understands your situation, as he, too, is facing tragedy and grief. His brother-in-law and sister live in France. He just received word from his sister that her husband was killed when he tried to escape from a train transporting him to a work camp in Germany.

"The doctor is very familiar with and has helped the French Resistance. He has also helped José on several occasions move French Jews and Allied airmen to the British Consulate. I know he has recently been in touch with the consulate regarding a Jewish boy fleeing the Germans. He will work behind the scenes and he will help you in your escape. Being injured, Marcel, may actually work to your advantage."

Doctor Casillas hurried into the room. "Marcel, I just talked with Doctor Ronaldo Torres, one of the chief surgeons at the hospital and a close friend of mine. I told him about you and your medical situation and that the French Resistance has brought you across the Pyrénées. He will help you at my urging.

"I have made arrangements to have an ambulance transport you, your friend, and José to the Donostia University Hospital tomorrow morning. Doctor Torres will be notified as soon as you arrive. He will arrange surgery sometime in the afternoon." Marcel brightened.

"Thank you for looking after me, Doctor Casillas. Father Sergio told me about your work with the French Resistance and that you know José. I am scared, and I am without my family, but I am grateful for the people I do have guiding me. I hope my fingers can be saved."

"José is a good friend, Marcel. I have worked with him and other Resistance fighters in the past. Hitler has the blood of so many innocents on his hands. I try to help the Allies whenever I am able. Stay calm, Marcel. Stay strong. You are young, able-bodied, and determined. Doctor Torres will take very good care of you. God bless and stay safe."

Twenty Five
March, 1944

Marcel's Amputation

O n March 23, 1944, close to noon, Marcel was taken to the emergency room of Donostia University Hospital in San Sabastián, Spain. The ambulance ride took just sixty minutes from Pamplona with lights flashing and siren blaring, mainly as a cover to protect the illegal immigrant passengers. Upon arrival, José and Leo extended well-wishes to Marcel as they exited the ambulance and walked the mile over to the British Consulate. As directed by Doctor Torres, the hospital attendants met the ambulance. They placed Marcel on a gurney and moved him into a rarely-used pre-surgical area. The nurses removed his mountain clothes, placed him in a hospital gown, and attached monitoring equipment. They then took x-rays of his left hand.

Doctor Torres and a nurse walked down the long corridor and approached Marcel. "Bonjour, Marcel. *Je suis Doctor Torres* (I am Doctor Torres). *Je parle français mal*" (I speak French poorly).

The nurse next to him, Maria Vilda, let Marcel know that she spoke French and would be the doctor's interpreter and medical assistant. Doctor Torres explained in rapid-fire medical terms, most of which Marcel did not understand, what was about to happen. He examined Marcel's hand and explained to him that the severe frostbite had caused necrosis, the premature death of cells in his fingers which could not be saved and must be amputated. He informed him that the surgery would take about four hours and that he would remain in the hospital for three or four days. The surgery would begin within the hour.

Coming out of sedation, Marcel drowsily watched the sun setting through the window of the hospital ward that consisted of twelve beds crowded together. As his brain began to clear, he contemplated the events of the day and its impact on his future. He was surprised that, at that moment, he had little pain. He was anxious to see the new formation of his hand, absent his pinky and ring finger.

Doctor Torres and Nurse Maria appeared at his bedside. Doctor Torres reassured Marcel that the operation was successful. He explained that after forty-eight hours they would begin physical therapy to avoid stiffness in his hand and fingers. Marcel asked the doctor when he would be released. "Complete healing usually takes three to four weeks, although hypersensitivity may remain longer. I am prescribing medication to control the pain. Barring any complications, you will be discharged in three or four days."

Early on Marcel's second day at the hospital, he was awakened by a tap on his shoulder. José was standing next to his bed. "Bonjour, Marcel! I just wanted to see how you are doing and say goodbye. I brought your rucksack. How are you feeling?"

Marcel sat up and raised his bandaged left hand. "Do you know the doctor had to take off two fingers? They are going to show me today what my hand looks like. So here I am with a war wound. The Nazis are responsible for this."

José flashed a weak smile and tried to soothe Marcel's feelings. "Marcel, I know that this is difficult, but remember, look ahead—never look back. Each day is a new beginning for you. Focus on your future which begins today. You are now safe and free from the German terror."

"I'm trying, José, but it is hard not to be angry. Hitler has taken everything from me, and now today you are saying goodbye? You said you would take me to the British Consulate. Where is Leo? What happens to me after I leave here?"

José found a folding chair and sat it next to Marcel's bed and placed his rucksack on the bed post. "Marcel, I must return to our Resistance group as quickly as possible. Your time here in the hospital is uncertain. I have discussed your situation with Doctor Torres. When he releases you, he will have Nurse Maria take you to the British Consulate, which is a short walk from here. When I dropped off Leo, I had a long conversation with their Associate Consul, William Higgins. Remember that name. He is expecting you and will make arrangements for you to travel to England as soon as possible.

"The war is escalating and there is talk of an Allied invasion into France within the coming months, so it is important to get you to England quickly. Spain is neutral, but in this war you never know where or when the bombings may occur. Leo will be staying at a boarding school in San Sabastián until the end of the conflict and then return to France.

"In your rucksack I have placed forms in an envelope that you will need when you arrive at the consulate. You will find some English currency in the envelope. Marcel, I told Higgins about the capture of Mark and Tim. He knows many of the Guardia military. He mentioned one name, General Ernesto Cortez, who has helped him obtain the release of other Allied soldiers. Since the United States entered the war, Cortez has also made strong connections with U.S. military. Higgins said that he will contact Cortez to see if he has any information about Tim and Mark."

"I am afraid I have lost them, too, José. I hope they can be found and can go back to England. Did you say that the British Consul will arrange for my travel to England? Will they place me in an orphanage or boarding school there?"

"Higgins did not tell me what will happen to you when you arrive in England. You will need to ask him. Just know, Marcel, that similar arrangements have been made for other orphan children that we have brought to Spain from France. I told Higgins that you are Catholic and that both your parents were killed by the Germans. He is anxious to assist you.

"I must say adieu now. Our Lady of Lourdes will continue to watch over you." José stood and bent over to give Marcel a kiss on his forehead.

"José, thank you for saving my life and helping me escape. Please stay safe. I will miss you."

On Marcel's third day in the hospital, Doctor Torres examined him and showed him the new configuration of his left hand. "Marcel, your hand is healing well and I had enough soft tissue to cover the bone of your knuckles. Your hand looks a bit smaller, but that will just be your new look." He smiled at Marcel.

"You tell me there is minimal pain and the nurse tells me that your fever is gone. You were very lucky we did the surgery when we did. Had we waited any longer the gangrene may have spread and you may have lost other fingers. The sutures in your hand should remain for a few more days. Tomorrow I will make arrangements to have you transported to the British Consulate."

Marcel looked at his hand. "Thank you Doctor Torres. My hand looks better than I thought it would. Three fingers will work for me. Who needs a small finger and ring finger anyway? I don't wear rings." Doctor Torres laughed.

"And you don't need ten fingers to play soccer or chess! I like your optimistic attitude!"

On Monday morning, March 27, 1944, Nurse Maria came to Marcel's bed. "Bonjour, Marcel. I hope you are well rested and your pain continues to subside. Doctor Torres asked me to walk with you to the British Consulate, but first we must find some clothing for you. We have a great amount of used clothes in our storeroom. We should be able to find a few items just your size.

"I also have some paperwork for you that Dr. Torres prepared for the Consul." Nurse Maria took Marcel's temperature. "Très bon! It is normal. You are ready to begin your new adventure!" Marcel shook his head.

"I don't think I am ready for another new adventure!"

In the storeroom, Marcel found two long-sleeved shirts, khaki pants, a belt, socks, shoes, and underwear. He found a dressing room and quickly changed. He put his old clothes in a large crate in back of the room and some of the new belongings into his rucksack. Nurse Maria and he exited the hospital and began the short walk to the British Consulate.

"Do you live here in San Sabastián?"

"Yes, and I love living here. The city sits on the banks of the Bay of Biscay. This is a large port city and we are close to France. We also enjoy three beautiful beaches. The last five years have been difficult with our own Spanish war and now the world war is having an impact on us as well. But I live with faith and hope."

As they walked, Marcel could hear the waves beating against the seawall. He thought that maybe this would be a nice place to live. Maria told him they were getting close to the Consulate. "Marcel, when we arrive, Doctor Torres told me to ask to see William Higgins. I have met him before. He is a very nice English gentleman who speaks Spanish and French. You will be in good hands."

Maria pointed to the brick and stone building with a humble façade at the end of the street. There was a British flag hanging near the large entrance. Marcel took a deep breath as they walked up the concrete steps. A British soldier was standing inside the front entrance. Maria told him that Consul William Higgins was expecting them. The guard asked them to take a seat, then walked over to the wall phone and made a call. In just a few minutes a tall, slender man in a blue suit came down the hall. Maria and Marcel stood to greet him, and Maria made introductions.

"Bonjour, Marcel. I have heard from your passeur, José, that you are seeking safe passage to England. Maria, it is very nice to see you again."

"And you as well." Maria mentioned Marcel's surgery to Higgins and the need to remove his sutures.

"He will be well cared for," Higgins said reassuringly. Marcel, let me show you to my office." Maria gave Marcel a kiss on both cheeks. "God speed and stay safe."

Marcel followed Higgins to his large office. "Please take a seat, Marcel. How are you feeling? I understand from Doctor Torres that two of your fingers were amputated. You must be very concerned and anxious to hear where your next stop will be and what I have planned for you."

Marcel looked into Higgins' dark, luminous eyes and knew that his life would be briefly in his hands. "Monsieur Higgins, thank you for helping me. I am thirteen and at this point, all I know is that I am an orphan with amputated fingers. I have no family, no friends. I miss my parents, my sister, and my life in France."

"Marcel, I have assisted several French children in similar circumstances, and I have seen the effects of the emotional and physical trauma this war has caused. You are a strong young man, and with my help, you will find a new life.

"We have a network of children's homes in England that take orphans who are fleeing Nazi-occupied Europe. I will be sending you to the Children's Home for Boys in Brighton, a beautiful English town located near the water. You will travel this evening on one of our naval ships, the HMS *Amethyst*. It is a new ship just launched last year. The navy uses it for anti-submarine and escort duties. It docked here in San Sabastián just yesterday and will deploy to Southampton, England. Your new home in Brighton is just a quick ride from the port. You will find several French children living there. There is an excellent school that will provide you with English language training. In a few months you will be speaking fluent English.

"I will create the necessary documents required for your travels. While you wait in my conference room I will have someone bring you a bite to eat. I know that I just dropped a great deal of information on your shoulders. Are there any questions you would like to ask me?"

"Will there be other children on this ship? How long will it take to sail to England?"

Higgins stood and walked over to Marcel. "Did Dr. Torres give you some papers to give to me?" Marcel opened his rucksack and found the envelope given to him by Maria and handed it to Higgins. "Thank you. These are the medical papers Dr. Torres prepared concerning your surgery. We have a doctor on board the ship. He will examine your hand and most likely remove your stitches. He will also be your guardian during your time on the ship. His name is Doctor Thomas Taylor. You will be in seclusion so you can catch up on your sleep. To your questions, you will be the only child on the ship. Sailing time to Southampton is about twenty-six hours depending on the weather and the waves. Have you ever sailed on a ship before?" Marcel said that he hadn't.

"So, Marcel, your journey continues." Marcel straightened his shoulders, encouraged by Higgins' reassurances.

"I think I am ready."

Twenty Six
April, 1944

Marcel's Voyage to England

Higgins and Marcel arrived at the San Sabastián dock late in the afternoon. Several large freighters were unloading cargo and crew. They walked along the pier toward the HMS *Amethyst*, passing several ships with their smoking stacks and cranes moving cargo from ship to pier. He saw sailors and crew in various uniforms with baggage in hand. The bustling pace seemed to energize him.

As they approached the *Amethyst*, Marcel stopped and pointed toward the ship. "It looks like my trip may be dangerous. I've never seen so many guns!"

"We are at war, Marcel, and this is one of England's many warships. Yes, once the ship is in international waters, there is always danger, especially from German submarines, but you will be in good hands with our naval crew. It is a quick ride from here to England, and a relatively safe route, so calm your fears. I dare say your walk across the Pyrénées was much more dangerous."

Higgins and Marcel held on to the handrails as they walked up the gangplank. An officer in a handsome naval uniform greeted Higgins as Marcel and he stepped onto the deck. Higgins spoke to him in English, handed him a large manila file folder, and then turned to Marcel.

"Marcel, please meet Doctor Thomas Taylor. He will be your companion as you sail to Southampton. You are now in very good hands, so I will say farewell. God speed!"

Marcel stared in awe at Dr. Taylor in his naval uniform and white cap. Taylor spoke excellent French. "Welcome aboard, Marcel. Captain James Boyce, our ship commander, sends his greetings to you. Follow me to your cabin where we can review your medical records and I can examine your hand. Tell me, how are you feeling?"

Marcel told Taylor that he was feeling well and followed him down a narrow winding staircase to the lower deck and then down the hallway, where Dr. Taylor opened the cabin door. Inside was a small room with a porthole, one chair, overhead closet, and a single bed. Marcel threw his rucksack on the bed and sat next to it as Dr. Taylor pulled over the chair. He carefully removed the bandage from Marcel's hand, looked at it thoroughly, and asked Marcel to move his fingers and hand.

"Everything is looking very good. Let me go and gather some medical supplies and I will give you a new bandage. I will not be long."

Taylor returned carrying his medical bag and began to wrap Marcel's hand when there was a loud knock on the door. Taylor opened the door to two soldiers dressed in English camouflage uniforms who waved and smiled at Marcel. He couldn't believe his eyes. He jumped off the bed and hugged them both, not wanting to let go.

"Doctor Taylor, these are the soldiers who crossed the Pyrénées with me. I thought they were captured by the Spanish soldiers and would be turned over to the Nazis and sent to Germany. I never thought that I would see them again. Would you please translate for us?"

The doctor translated as Marcel's voice shook with emotion. "José, Leo, and I prayed so hard for your safety and return. Another miracle has happened!"

Tim ruffled Marcel's hair. "It was a miracle, and now we are sailing to England, just like you."

Marcel showed Mark and Tim his hand before Dr. Taylor finished bandaging it. The airmen described what happened to them when they were captured by the Spanish Guardia near Sangüesa. They were arrested and taken to a military camp where they were questioned for several hours and then placed in a cell, believing that the Spanish Guardia would return them to France and hand them over to the Nazis. They were shocked when they were taken to San Sabastián and brought to the *Amethyst*.

They asked about Leo. Marcel told them that he was placed in a boarding school in San Sabastián and that he himself was going to an orphanage in Brighton, England.

Tim said that he and Mark would be flying again within the next few weeks and that Southampton was full of U.S. military preparing for an invasion of France. "Marcel, a new phase of this war is about to begin. Hitler is about to receive his reckoning. You stay safe."

"We are so glad we got to see you, Marcel," said Mark. "Maybe we will see you again when we reach Southampton."

"I hope so!" All three hugged again and said their goodbyes.

Marcel still couldn't believe they were on the same ship and that they survived their arrest. He thanked Doctor Taylor for his translation. "My pleasure, Marcel. In wartime there are so many unexplained happenings, both good and bad. I am glad I got to witness one of the good!

"I will have some food brought to your room, and tomorrow morning I will remove your sutures. Try to get some rest."

Though the seas were rough, the *Amethyst* moved at a rapid pace. Marcel enjoyed the view from his porthole and saw a large flotilla of warships moving in and out of a distant port which he believed to be Southampton. Doctor Taylor arrived early and removed Marcel's stitches and examined his hand. "Marcel, your hand is healing and you are well on the way to recovery. Be very careful with it, though, over the next few months. We will dock in about three hours, so stay in your room until I return."

Marcel looked at his hand, absent his bandage, and flexed his hand and fingers. "Can you tell me what happens when I arrive?"

Doctor Taylor handed him a folder with some writing on the front. "This envelope contains information about you, and you are to give it to the person meeting you at the dock. Let me tell you about the Southampton port.

"The Germans were not kind to the people of Southampton. Bombs started to fall here in June of 1940 and continued until the spring of 1942. They didn't just bomb our shipyards, docks and railway lines, but also schools, churches, and homes. Hundreds of civilians, including children, were killed. Now it is the place for the Allied troops to mobilize for a future invasion into Europe, most likely France. You will only be in Southampton a few hours, and then you will be transported by car to Brighton, which is where the Children's Home for Boys is located.

"Brighton is still recovering as well. The latest air attack there was on May 25 of last year. The Luftwaffe dropped twenty-two bombs, killing men, women and children. You will see much destruction as you travel into the city, but the area where your new home will be received little damage. You will also be about forty-five miles from London.

"Gather your things now. We will soon be in port and I will return to take you to the pier. Now you will begin your English journey."

Just before noon, the whistles and sirens on the ship sounded loud and sharp, signaling disembarkation. From his porthole Marcel watched as the gangplank was moved into place and sailors crowded onto the pier. He thought he saw Mark and Tim in different uniforms from the group of British sailors surrounding them, and remembered how worried he was about them and how fortunate he was to have met two American airmen.

Doctor Taylor knocked on the cabin door. "It's time to go, Marcel. We are not going down the main gangway. Officers use another exit on the rear of the cruiser. Let me check your hand one last time. Here is something for you to remember your time on the *Amethyst.*"

He handed Marcel a small model of the ship sitting neatly in a box with HMS *AMETHYST* printed across the side panel. Marcel was touched by the gesture.

"Thank you, Doctor Taylor, for the gift and for taking care of me. This will always remind me of your kindness."

They walked through the narrow halls and steel stairways in silence except for the sound of their echoing footsteps and the opening of the metal door that took them to a stairway and out to the pier. They moved along the busy pier until they came to a crowded parking lot. As they reached the curb, a large, black Austin Six sedan pulled up next to them, a small sign taped to the rear window: Children's Home for Boys. The driver opened his door, walked over to Marcel and Taylor, extended one hand to Dr. Taylor, and placed the other hand on Marcel's shoulder. "Good day. I am Joseph Prucha. I work at the Home for Boys and will be your driver." He pulled an identification card from his wallet and showed it to Dr. Taylor.

Dr. Taylor provided Prucha with pertinent information about his new passenger, including that Marcel spoke very little English.

"Then please tell this fine young man that I will be picking up one other child before we head to Brighton, which is a ride of about ninety minutes." Dr. Taylor translated and gave Marcel a warm embrace. "All the best to you, Marcel. Please remember me in your prayers." Dr. Taylor opened the door and Marcel got into the back seat with his rucksack in tow. Marcel waved goodbye to Dr. Taylor. *Another goodbye in my life*, he thought, as the Austin pulled away.

Prucha skillfully maneuvered through the crowded streets of Southampton. Marcel gazed out the window, taking in the sights and sounds of the militarized city. He saw some of the remaining destruction from the bombs dropped by the Luftwaffe. Prucha pulled the Austin behind a small, two-story building with a sign across the front door: *YMCA*. He left the motor running as he entered the building, returning with a young boy and a woman dressed in a nurse's uniform.

The boy moved into the back seat next to Marcel holding a small travel bag. The nurse sat up front. As Prucha eased back into the traffic, the nurse turned her head and looked at Marcel. "Bonjour. *Je m'appelle Nurse Charlotte*" (My name is Nurse Charlotte). Marcel was surprised and pleased to hear her speaking French. She told him that she was born in Paris and moved to England just before the Germans invaded in 1940.

Marcel introduced himself and told her about his amputation. The young boy next to him reached over and touched Marcel's hand.

Nurse Charlotte explained to Marcel that the child next to him was Charles, and that he was being transferred to the Children's Home. "His parents and two siblings were killed in the spring of 1942 during one of the German air attacks on

Southampton. The YMCA cared for him for almost a year and now he will be finding a new home at the Brighton orphanage." Marcel sat in silence and wondered how many orphans this war had created.

Twenty Seven
June, 1944

Another New Beginning

Marcel settled into his new residence along with over thirty other boys. His unit of ten boys was for the older youth, ages thirteen to eighteen. The staff primarily consisted of ten men who watched over them and provided instruction. There were also two nurses. The food was tasty and plentiful, and everyone was kind and caring. The headmaster, Mr. David Mercer, wanted to give each child a feeling of security along with an understanding that the boys were loved and valued.

Marcel had his own small bed and took a hot shower on Saturdays. He already had one medical checkup, and a doctor had stopped by to check on his hand. Several of the more curious boys asked about his amputation. Marcel met one staff member who spoke French and two of the boys in his unit spoke French as well. Also, he enjoyed conversations with Nurse Charlotte who reminded him of his mother. They shared stories of France. He was especially interested in hearing about her relatives who lived in Lourdes.

The weather in this part of England was still cool and most of the flowers would not bud until June. Marcel enjoyed the gardens that surrounded the orphanage. The leaves and blossoms on the trees were beginning to show signs of springtime color. He was assigned various work activities: cleaning the bathrooms, sorting the wash, and helping in the kitchen, but the one he enjoyed most was weeding and tending to the garden, as it brought back nostalgic memories of the garden behind the bakery in Lourdes. He remembered how his mother would paint in the gazebo while Nicole and he would play. He remembered how much his mother loved flowers. He sometimes wondered if someone salvaged his mother's paintings.

During the week he took classes in English, art, history, and, with the help of his two new French-speaking friends, Cameron and Roger, algebra. One class Marcel especially enjoyed was World Events. During every class, the instructor, Mr. David Ebert, passed around a copy of the *London Times* and they discussed what was happening as the war continued.

One of the headlines, "140 Lancasters Bomb Factory in Toulouse," caught Marcel's attention, and he asked Cameron to help him read through the story. They learned that on April 6, a German aircraft factory was targeted and destroyed and many civilians were killed. Marcel remembered Toulouse as being a beautiful city on the banks of the River Garonne where his father had visited. He thought about Nicole in her new home and prayed that she was safe from the bombings. The story was upsetting to him because it confronted him with the fact that the war was still raging close to his former home.

In early May, American and Canadian soldiers visited the orphanage on the weekends and brought the children candy treats and other goodies. The older boys loved the Bazooka bubble gum and the M&M chocolates. On special occasions, the soldiers would bring fudge brownies and cupcakes for everyone, stuffed animals for the younger boys, and soccer balls for the older children. In early June, Marcel wondered why the soldiers stopped visiting.

On Wednesday morning, June 7, 1944, Mr. Ebert announced and confirmed to the class what they had been hearing: that on Tuesday, June 6, more than 160,000 Allied troops landed along a fifty-mile stretch of heavily-fortified French coastline to fight Nazi Germany on the beaches of Normandy, France. He read to the class a front page story that appeared in the *London Times*. In part, it read:

The invasion of Normandy was the largest amphibious assault ever launched. It involved 5 army divisions in the initial assault and over 7,000 ships. In addition, there were 11,000 aircraft.

In total, 75,215 British and Canadian troops and 57,500 US troops were landed by sea on D-Day. Another 23,400 were landed by air.

There was an intense class discussion about how this invasion would favorably affect the outcome of the war. When an eighteen-year-old announced to the class that he would be leaving the orphanage at the end of the month to enter the British Army, everyone was stunned.

Marcel wondered how this news would impact Diop, José, and all of the Resistance fighters who were still fighting the Germans in France. He remembered the excitement in the camp when they were told that General Charles de Gaulle was working with the British military to accelerate the air drops of weapons, including machine guns and grenade launchers. General de Gaulle strongly supported their Resistance unit. Marcel continued to pray for their safety and hoped that someday they would reunite.

On Wednesday, August 2, 1944, the class heard that the Germans launched 316 V-1 flying bombs on London, the highest single day total yet. Mr. Ebert told them that over a hundred bombs reached the capital, with some hitting the Tower Bridge. Many civilians, including children, died in the bombings. Mr. Ebert explained to those boys who were new to England that Brighton was only seventy-seven miles from London. "Boys, we have been lucky so far, but the war still rages, so if you hear the air raid sirens, take shelter immediately."

It seemed as if every day in Marcel's World History class brought more good news from France. The Allies seemed to be successful in their efforts to free France from German occupation. On Friday, August 25, Mr. Ebert brought more good news to the French boys in the class. Ebert shared the article, "Germans Surrender Paris," with the boys.

The commander of the German garrison of Paris surrenders the city to Lieutenant Henri Karcher of the French 2nd Armored Division. The surrender encompasses five thousand German soldiers, fifty artillery pieces, and a company of tanks under German command.

Ebert reminded the class that along with the Paris surrender, the German garrison at Lourdes also surrendered on August 19. Ebert addressed the French boys in his class. "It looks like the war in France is coming to a close after four years of German occupation. I am sure this news brings a bit of happiness to each of you." The boys jumped up and cheered in excitement while the rest of the class applauded and gave them the "V" sign.

The summer passed by quickly and the boys were told that there would be no classes during the month of September. Marcel was pleased with the progress he had made in his English class. Cameron and Roger tutored him in vocabulary and spelling. He was beginning to understand the conversations among the English boys in his class.

On the first Saturday of September, the headmaster surprised them with a bus trip to the Brighton Palace Pier, a large amusement park with a pier that extended into the English Channel. It was a beautiful, cloudless day for the excursion. Each of the ten boys on the trip received three English pounds for spending money. Marcel told Cameron and Roger that he was only going to speak English on this excursion. They both laughed, and Cameron said in French, "Oh yes—until you see something on the menu that you can't read!"

This was Marcel's first visit to an amusement park. He was anxious to sample as many rides as possible. The day was packed with fun and he, along with Cameron and Roger, walked the long pier and rode the Ferris wheel, the roller coaster, and the bumper cars. Even though Cameron and Roger teased him about being too old, he rode the merry-go-round with great delight. They also rolled up their pants and walked along the beach as they savored their ice cream cones. It was the most fun he had had since his parents, Nicole, and he had gone to the circus. That seemed like such a long time ago.

The month of September, 1944 saw the boys play soccer and rugby and gather on Sunday evenings to listen to the BBC radio broadcast music and a few comedy shows. Prior to the start of the broadcast at 7 p.m., Headmaster Mercer would stop by to speak with the boys to see if any were in distress or just wanted to engage him in conversation. Marcel always took this opportunity to speak with him. He was worried about his future, and Mr. Mercer would assure him that the future of all the boys was his main priority.

On one occasion, Mr. Mercer wanted to speak privately with Marcel. "Marcel, I would like to discuss with you the possibility of sending several of you boys to the United States. I have already talked with Cameron and Roger, and they are very interested, so I would like us all to meet in my office tomorrow to talk about this further."

Astonished, Marcel asked in English, "Mr. Mercer, are you telling me that I may be going to the United States?"

"Yes, Marcel, and your perfect English indicates that you may be ready! But let's discuss it tomorrow."

The following day, Mr. Mercer met with Marcel, Cameron, and Roger in his office. He explained to the boys in great detail about an organization he was working with, the Children's Overseas Reception Board (CORB). He told them that CORB helped orphan children emigrate from England to Canada, Australia, New Zealand, South Africa, and the United States. CORB notified Mr. Mercer that they have transport available for several children to sail from Southampton to the United States on Sunday October 15. Once they arrived in the U.S. they would be transferred to an orphanage in New York City.

Their headmaster strongly encouraged the boys to accept this invitation. "This will be, for each of you, a new life in a new country. The United States offers democracy, freedom, safety, and so much opportunity. I am not demanding that you travel there. This is your decision to make. How does each of you feel about this?"

Marcel and Cameron replied that they would accept the offer. "Will we stay together at the same orphanage once we arrive in the United States?" Cameron asked. Mr. Mercer nodded.

"Yes, you will reside at the Guardian Angel Orphanage in Brooklyn, New York, a Catholic home run by the Sisters of Mercy. I have sent several boys there, and I keep in touch with them. Their letters tell me that it is an excellent environment and that they have a good school."

Mercer looked at Roger. "Roger, how do you feel about traveling to the United States and beginning a new life there?"

"My parents and brother were killed just six months ago by German bombs. But I have uncles and aunts living in Wales, so I am hoping that I can go live there. Marcel and Cameron are in a very different situation. I wish them well, but I will stay here."

"I understand, Roger. Each of you must decide what is in your best interest. Cameron and Marcel, I will complete your travel documents and notify staff in the States of your plans. There will be a total of fifteen children sailing on the *Marco Polo* from Southampton to Ellis Island, New York. The other children will be from orphanages around England. You will have one suitcase, medical records, and a CORB identification card. You will be busy between now and your departure date."

The headmaster walked over to his bookcase and brought back several books about U.S. history, maps of New York City, and several issues of *LIFE* magazine. "Take these. They should help you to gain a better understanding of your new country."

Twenty Eight
October, 1944

Welcome to America

On this cloudy fall morning, Cameron and Marcel waited at the front entrance of the Children's Home for Boys for Mr. Prucha to drive them to the Southampton harbor for their transport to the United States. They had gotten little sleep the night before, staying up late after packing, looking at the magazines, and spending their last hours reminiscing with Roger about their time together at the orphanage. They vowed to stay in touch.

On the drive to the harbor, Prucha told them that he visited the United States and the city of Baltimore ten years ago to visit his grandfather. While he was there he took the train to New York City to visit other relatives. He told the boys he liked New York with all of its museums and department stores, but that the most impressive landmark was the Statue of Liberty located on Bedloe's Island in New York Harbor.

"You should be able to see the statue as soon as your ship enters New York Harbor. It is such a thrilling thing to see!

Your cruise to New York should take about ten days." Prucha pulled into the designated parking area where he saw the sign, "Children's Overseas Reception Board."

"This is your assembly spot. Have a good trip, and I hope wonderful opportunities await you in America. God be with you!"

"Thank you, Mr. Prucha!"

The boys scrambled out of the car, barely able to contain their excitement. They saw an older man with gray hair and glasses, dressed in a blue suit, standing with several other children. There was a small round tag on his lapel, on which was printed CORB. Cameron and Marcel handed him one of the forms given to them by Headmaster Mercer.

"Are you the person who will take us to the United States?" Marcel asked. The man smiled broadly. "Yes. My name is Mr. Thomas Waterhouse, and I will be with you for the duration of the voyage. We should be boarding in just a bit, so stay close."

Soon the *Marco Polo* lowered its gangplank and the passengers began to board. Waterhouse gathered the fifteen children around him. There were ten boys and five girls ranging in age from seven to fifteen. "Everyone stay close and follow me." He led them down several flights of steps into the lowest level of the ship. Most of the crew had cabins on the bottom level. He pointed to a small dining hall before leading them down nine more steps.

Waterhouse stopped next to a set of double doors and raised his arm. "All the boys gather in single file. All the girls stand here next to the wall." He opened the door and the boys walked into a small narrow room where ten cots were lined against the walls, almost on top of each other. Three portholes brightened the dimly lit room in the very bottom of the ship. They could hear the roar of the engines and smell the fuel. Waterhouse told the boys to place their suitcases under the cots.

"There is a toilet at the end of the hall. Sorry boys, no shower, but there is a faucet and sink behind that curtain. I will find some glasses. Get yourselves situated while I show the girls to their room."

Marcel and Cameron jumped on two cots close to one of the portholes. Marcel looked with disgust at Cameron. "Can you believe we will live like this for the next ten days? These are horrible conditions, but I guess we shouldn't complain. I hope we have lunch soon." Cameron sat up on his cot.

"We'll survive—I brought my little chess set! Just don't get seasick. Hopefully our lives are taking another step forward."

Mr. Waterhouse found ways to occupy the younger children to get them through the long hours. He provided some books and games and took them on little excursions around the ship. The older boys were allowed to access the promenade deck where they enjoyed the sunsets and watched the moon rise and cast its beam along the deck. One evening Marcel and Cameron discussed their future in America, and Marcel said he had been thinking about Roger.

"Do you think Roger made the right decision about not coming to America?" Cameron nodded his head.

"Yes, I think he did because he has family in Wales and he hopes he will reunite with them. My situation is different. I am fourteen and have been in an orphanage since I was twelve, so I watched the war from the orphanage outside of London. I heard the bombs, saw the fire, and tasted the smoke. I lived in fear, day after day. My father was a seaman and I was told he died when a German U-boat torpedoed his ship. About six months later, my mother died from cancer. I am an only child and I have no close relatives, but I was told my mother had family who lived in Pennsylvania. Maybe someday I will locate them. So I am hopeful. Our headmaster kept telling us that America is the land of promise and opportunity. I pray that we find both."

Marcel looked over the railing at the rising moon. "My horror began on April 19 of last year. My father and mother owned a bakery in Lourdes, France. On that Monday morning they came to arrest my mother because her father was Jewish. There was a scuffle and the Nazis murdered my father and arrested my mother. She later died in a German concentration camp. My sister and I found our way to an orphanage. A nice couple adopted my sister. It was getting too dangerous to stay at the orphanage, so when the opportunity came for me to escape, I took it. I crossed the Pyrénées to Spain and then sailed to England." He raised his left hand. "I told you the rest of the story about my amputation. Our lives have changed so quickly."

Cameron felt the chill of the ocean air. "Marcel, our lives can only get better. But no one has mentioned that there still is a threat of Nazi U-boats as we sail on to New York. Maybe it is safer for passenger ships than for cargo ships, but I am still worried. We could be a target." Marcel took a deep breath. "That is so true, but we are halfway there. Let's keep praying."

The boys spent their days reading books and magazines, playing chess and checkers, completing cross-word puzzles, and challenging each other to push-ups. The evening before they were to disembark, Mr. Waterhouse explained what they were to expect when they arrived in New York.

"Tomorrow at eight in the morning, we will be docking in New York Harbor. A ferry will take you to Ellis Island where you will have a medical check and go through legal processing. You will also have your suitcase inspected. The entire process will take about three hours. When all of that is completed, the ferry will take you back to the harbor where a bus will transport you to your assigned destination. Tomorrow is the day, children, when you will enter a new country and a new life. Have a good night's sleep, and I will see you in the morning."

On Wednesday, October 24, 1944, the *Marco Polo* lumbered into New York Harbor with the help of two tug boats. Waterhouse gathered all of the children along the upper deck to take in the view. Just as Mr. Prucha had promised, the Statue of Liberty stood tall and stately and welcoming. Marcel caught his breath and tears sprang to his eyes. *I wish Maman and Papa could see this.*

It was cool and windy, and the children were not dressed for the weather. They shivered from both the cold and the excitement. Waterhouse gathered them around him and told them that the statue represented the universal symbols of freedom, opportunity, and global friendship. He recited the most famous line from Emma Lazarus' poem that she wrote to raise money to construct the pedestal: "'Give me your tired, your poor, your huddled masses yearning to breathe free...'

"When you visit the statue, you will see the poem emblazoned on the pedestal. This is your history lesson for today." A few of the children waved at Lady Liberty as the ship moved into the harbor.

After the *Marco Polo* docked, Waterhouse led the children off the ship and onto the pier. Once again he gathered the children around him. "I will walk you down the pier and over to the ferry which will take us to Ellis Island. You will be handed many important paper forms. Be careful with them. I will be sitting at a small desk near the door. Once your processing has been completed, come over to me. When everyone is finished, we will take the ferry back to New York Harbor."

The room was very crowded with uniformed men and woman shouting orders in different languages. Cameron and Marcel stayed together as they moved from one line to the next. By late afternoon, all of the children had made their way back to Waterhouse, who surprised them with bags of pretzels. "I know you all must be very hungry. This should tide you over until dinner." The children chatted and ate their pretzels on the way to the ferry terminal.

There was a brief wait until the next ferry arrived. Waterhouse walked them onto the top deck for the ride back to the harbor. Once off the ferry, the children saw several buses of different colors lined up in the parking area. For the last time the children gathered around Waterhouse as he retrieved his roster from his bag and called out each of their names, their designated orphanage, and their bus color.

"Cameron and Marcel—Guardian Angel Orphanage—blue bus!" One by one the children boarded their buses, excited, anxious, and sad all at once. Waterhouse called after them, "Take care, stay safe, and welcome to the United States of America!" The children waved goodbye and blew kisses out the windows.

Waterhouse stood alone and watched the buses pull out of the lot, all heading in different directions. *Fifteen children,* he thought, *about to begin new chapters in their book of life. War orphans hoping for another chance to be loved.* Then he turned and headed out to Manhattan Street, deciding to walk for a while before going home.

Twenty Nine
October, 1944

Marcel Finds a New Home

The ride to Brooklyn was only four miles from the New York Harbor. The bus pulled into the parking area behind the Guardian Angel Orphanage. Cameron, Marcel, and two other boys stood outside with their suitcases and waited for someone to meet them. Soon a sister in a black habit and white cornette approached the bus. She spoke almost in a whisper. "Hello and God bless. I am Sister Mary Luke. Welcome to all of you. Each of you will be registered and given your room assignments, but first I have some dinner for you." The excitement of being in New York waned for Marcel as the thought of being in another orphanage weighed on his mind. *Dear God, how long will I stay here?*

Marcel settled nonetheless into the daily routine. His English continued to improve. He was back in class and remained close with Cameron. They bunked together and enjoyed the social interaction with the other boys. All of the boys came to know the chief administrator, Father Charles Garrison.

Father Charles was also their counselor and spent time with the thirteen-to-eighteen-year-old boys several hours a week. He was their cheerleader, gave them advice, and helped the boys establish goals. Father worked with them during their emotional struggles so each could reach his potential. He also was a liaison for families who expressed a desire to become foster parents or to adopt. Father Charles was aware that many children arriving at the orphanage were from England and other war-torn European countries, as he frequently interacted with the CORB organization.

In several of his conversations with Marcel he learned that, despite the trauma Marcel had experienced, he was well-adjusted and expressed a strong desire to find a permanent loving home and family. Looking directly at Father Charles, Marcel said, in a clear but emotional voice, "The war destroyed my family. I always thought we would spend a lifetime together, but the Nazis destroyed everything I loved. I have to face that my family and my home in Lourdes are gone. But I am still here and I am alive, and I pray that I can find a new family who will love me."

"Marcel, I am committed to helping all of you find loving families who will give you the opportunity for a new life and a new start."

Father Charles let the boys know that on the second Saturday in December the orphanage would be conducting an open house for those families who had expressed an interest in foster care and adoption. He explained to the boys that all of those attending had been screened, and that only those meeting the orphanage, as well as the State of New York's, very high standards were invited. Father called it a "meet and greet" event where everyone could get to know each other. He also told them the boys' choral group would sing Christmas carols and there would be food and punch.

The day arrived and several of the boys, including Marcel and Cameron, were asked to set up the large dining hall for the arrival of their guests. Some additional tables and chairs were set in place and two large sofas were moved behind the buffet line. Each child wore a tag stating his name, age, and birth country and carried an index card with a biographical summary. Father Charles informed the boys that he was expecting twenty to thirty adults.

At noon the guests started to arrive. The boys hung up their coats and took the guests to their seats. By twelve-thirty, most of the guests were mingling. Father Charles moved to the middle of the room. He welcomed the group and told them about the history of the Guardian Angel Orphanage. He introduced several of the nuns whom he asked to attend. Several people were taking notes, and Father Charles could sense their anticipation.

Father talked about the devastating impact the war in Europe had on families and the importance of foster care and adoption. "This is your opportunity to meet the children, really get to know them, tell them all about you, where you live and worship, and answer the children's questions. I have told them not to be shy. I will be here to answer your questions. Feel free to approach me at any time. Enjoy your afternoon with us!"

The food and drinks were served and the children moved from table to table. The room was filled with laughter, tears, and intense conversation. Marcel talked to several families from New York, Pennsylvania, and Rhode Island. He was sitting at an empty table eating his sandwich when a couple walked over to him and asked if they could sit with him. Marcel hurriedly put his napkin to his mouth. "Yes, please be seated. My name is Marcel."

The man spoke first. "Well hello, Marcel. My name is George Whiteford and this is my wife, Mary. We are from Maryland, a state not far from here." They told him that they lived on a forty-acre farm which kept them very busy. "We don't have children and would like to adopt. The pastor at the church we attend told us about the Children's Overseas Reception Board and the Guardian Angel Orphanage. That information connected us to Father Charles and brought us here today."

Mary looked at Marcel's tag. "I see that you are from Lourdes, France. My grandmother was born in Lyon, so I have some French blood. I also studied the French language in high school. Please tell us about yourself." Marcel told them his story of horror at the hands of the Nazis, the death of his mother and father, the adoption of his sister, and the trek across the Pyrénées that resulted in the loss of his fingers. "That was the last thing that was taken from me."

The couple listened intently, wondering how this young boy had survived through so much suffering. They both had tears in their eyes. George cleared his throat and complimented Marcel on his English and asked about his studies and sports.

"I really enjoy history, and I'm pretty good at soccer. Chess is my favorite game to play. Do you play chess?"

"No, Marcel, I don't play the game, but would love to learn if someone would teach me." Marcel sipped his drink and thought for a moment.

"I am a good teacher, and I think I might like to live on a farm."

The Whitefords spent the rest of their afternoon with Marcel. Father Charles ambled over to their table. "It looks like you have been enjoying each other's company. The concert is about to begin, but if you would like, I could meet with the three of you a bit later today." George and Mary both smiled with excitement. "Yes, Father, if you could meet with us, we do have some questions for you and Marcel. We are spending the night in New York and will drive home tomorrow."

George, Mary, and Marcel sat together and enjoyed the concert. Marcel glanced across the room and saw Cameron sitting with the couple he had been talking to most of the afternoon. Cameron smiled and waved. *Maybe our prayers have been answered*, Marcel thought, *and both of us have found a new family who will love us.*

The afternoon gathering was drawing to a close as Father Charles approached George and Mary and asked if they would like to come to his office so he could address their questions and perhaps discuss next steps. Encouraged by the prospect, they asked if Marcel could join them. Mary held Marcel's hand as the three of them followed Father to his office.

Father walked over to his file cabinet and found the paperwork that the Whitefords had submitted prior to their arrival. As they sat around a large work table, Father found his glasses and reviewed the file. "Just to let you know, I received this heart-warming letter from your pastor at St. Ignatius Church in Hickory. He stated that you are active members of the parish and spoke highly of both of you."

"Father, it seems that all of this is moving too fast, but in just a few brief hours, George and I have fallen in love with Marcel and we think he feels the same way."

Father looked at Marcel. "So tell me, Marcel, what are your thoughts?"

Marcel took a deep breath. "My head is spinning. I have been praying for a miracle and I think it just happened. This has been an exciting afternoon and there seems to be a closeness and affection that I can't describe. I would truly love to join Mr. and Mrs. Whiteford, if they will have me?"

"Marcel, Mary and I thought we were going to have lots of questions for Father Charles and you, but you just answered all of the ones we had for you. Now our only question for Father Charles is, what is the next step?"

Father gathered his thoughts and looked through the file. He found the forms that the Whitefords needed to complete. "The path from foster care to adoption is not that daunting, considering the circumstances in Marcel's case. Since both birth parents are deceased, foster care can happen quickly. There are forms that I will need to complete, and I will do that in the morning, but you can take these and complete them at your hotel this evening. Let's meet here in my office at 10:00 tomorrow morning, and if everything is in order, Marcel can leave with you. Just so you know, the adoption process varies from state to state but usually takes about eighteen months. I have contacts in Maryland who will assist you to assure that all the legal requirements are in order. How does that sound?"

Mary looked at George and Marcel and began to cry. "I have been praying so hard for this moment. Marcel, George and I will surround you with love. You have completed our lives, and we hope we can offer you a special place to begin the process of completing yours."

"This is a big step for all of you," said Father. "I have placed many children over the years, and I have to say that this one feels especially right and good. I can see it in your faces and hear it in your voices." Father stood and walked over to Marcel and placed his hand on his shoulder. "Marcel, you are going to be in good stead with a beautiful family living on a farm in Maryland. The Lord does watch over us and answers our prayers."

Following handshakes and hugs and a quick conversation between Marcel and the Whitefords, Marcel said goodbye and walked to his room. He was filled with excitement and couldn't wait to tell Cameron.

"So, Marcel," said Cameron, putting down the book he was reading and sitting up on his bed, "Tell me what is happening! Are you going to be in foster care?" Beaming, Marcel told Cameron all about the Whitefords, their farm, and that he will be leaving with them tomorrow. "They asked how I would feel about being called Marc instead of Marcel. I told them that I was ready to start a new life, and that Marc suited me just fine."

Cameron was excited for Marcel, but he told him he was going to miss him and that he wasn't sure about his own future.

"The couple I spent the afternoon with seemed to like me. They said they would need more time and would come back next weekend to take me Christmas shopping in New York. They live in Philadelphia, so it's not so far away. I really liked them. Time will tell." Marcel sat next to Cameron on the bed and put his arm around his shoulders.

"Cameron, I will miss you too, my friend. Let's promise to keep in touch."

Thirty
January, 1945

Marcel Longs to See His Sister

Marc was settling in with his foster parents at the Eagle Wings Farm in northern Harford County, Maryland. The farm, with its beautiful rolling fields, was nestled along the banks of Deer Creek. Marc could feel the bonds of love and family forming and strengthening around him. The Whitefords celebrated their first family Christmas together with Marc, following midnight Mass at St. Ignatius Church.

While in the comfort of his bedroom, Marc was deep in thought and remembered something he read at the orphanage: *Home is a feeling, not a place—a feeling created by love, connection, enjoyment, reflection.* Marc was feeling that he finally had rediscovered a home—a home where his life could begin again, where he could rediscover the love he once felt in Lourdes with his mother, father and sister.

Winter brought a slower pace to the farm, allowing George to spend more time with Marc, who welcomed the chores and loved the animals and driving the tractor. He enjoyed fishing and was teaching George how to play chess and kick a soccer ball. Helping Mary in the kitchen, especially when she was baking, was one of his favorite things to do.

On Saturdays, Mary prepared a farmhouse breakfast. Marc brought in fresh milk from one of the cows, and Mary prepared pancakes with blueberries when they were in season. Honey, fruit jams, and homemade bread were always on the table, evoking the fragrance of summer. George made the coffee and fried the bacon.

On these special mornings, George and Mary encouraged Marc to tell them all about his life in France. He shared stories of his childhood and the family bakery in Lourdes. He liked to reminisce about his sister and tell stories of their childhood together. He also told them about Diop—how he immigrated to France from Cameroon and how the Lourdes water caused the miraculous recovery from his illness.

Mary told Marc that she would like to take him to France after the war was over and Europe had recovered. "Hopefully, we can locate your sister, Nicole, and have a reunion of family and friends!"

Mary had several meetings with the county school officials concerning proper grade assignment, and Marc took several placement tests. A decision was made to place Marc in the eighth grade. At age fourteen, he would be somewhat older than most of the children at that grade level, but Marc understood that he must accept the decision made. School started at the beginning of January, and he was making new friends.

Most evenings after dinner, George turned on the radio, and Marc and he listened to the world news and sports. The news always began with an update on the war, both in Europe and the Pacific. George was very interested in the war; he had a brother serving in the Army in Europe. Marc always was attentive, hoping he would hear something about France. In late January, Marc heard that the Soviet troops had liberated the Auschwitz and Birkenau concentration camps, where they discovered thousands of prisoners barely alive and thousands of bodies in makeshift graves.

Marc thought back to 1943 and the Christmas concert at the orphanage in Tarbes. He remembered when Mother Anne Marie gave Nicole and him the worst possible news: the news of their mother's death in Auschwitz. That name, Auschwitz, would always burn with great sadness in his heart. Later that evening, as he prepared for bed, he looked for the prayer book that his mother and father gave him on his First Communion day. He found it at the bottom of his well-worn rucksack. In the middle of the book he saw the folded note handed to him by Mother Anne Marie.

He carefully unfolded it and read again the message sent by one of his mother's prison friends:

With great sadness, I am informing you that Josette is no longer with us. She traveled on angel's wings to visit our Heavenly Father on November 19. She died from typhus at Auschwitz.
Her friend, Viviane

He walked down the steps and found George and Mary sitting on the sofa. He walked over and sat between them. "I know I told you that my mother died at Auschwitz in November of 1943. When I heard the news tonight that Auschwitz was liberated, I thought of her and wanted to show you the note my sister and I received at the orphanage. It is written in French so I will read it to you." The words were blurred by his tears, but he knew them by heart.

"The Nazis killed my father and then my mother. Nicole and I cannot visit them at a cemetery, and we will never know what happened to their bodies. All we will ever have are fading memories." Mary and George embraced Marc. Mary looked at the note in Marc's hand and folded his fingers over it.

"This will always be a family treasure for you and your sister. Thank you for sharing it with us. Keep it safe."

"Marc, please know how much Mary and I love you, and that you can come to us anytime with your sorrows. We know you have been surrounded by so much heartache and sadness."

Marc enjoyed his days more and more on the farm. He was up by four-thirty every morning taking care of the animals and helping George with various chores, then doing more farm work when he returned from his school day. He enjoyed dinner with George and Mary and their conversations about the business of the farm. They always wanted an update on his school day.

George liked to talk about world events, and on this April night they discussed the death of President Roosevelt. "I can't believe the Lord took him at this critical time for the country and the world. I know he had health issues, but he was only sixty-three. Now we will have to see how Truman can bring an end to this war."

A few weeks later, on May 7, 1945, the news broke that Germany had surrendered at Allied headquarters in Reims, France. The war in Europe had ended. The Whitefords celebrated around the dinner table with wine for Mary and George and a ginger ale for Marc. The three raised their glasses, and George gave a toast, "To victory in Europe!"

"Here, here!" they chanted.

"Now Truman has to get the Japanese to surrender."

Just a few months later, on August 14, 1945, victory over Japan was celebrated following the dropping of atomic bombs on Hiroshima and Nagasaki on August 6 and 9, respectively. The death toll was over eighty thousand. The horribly tragic world war was finally over.

For Marc, the next two years of his life in Maryland were rewarding and full of milestones. He turned sixteen on May 6,

1947, and started high school, where he played varsity soccer and met his first girlfriend. He was making good marks in his classes. He was legally adopted by the Whitefords, and growing to love more and more his new family and home and life on the farm. He memorized the saying by Thomas Jefferson that George had framed and placed on the wall in the kitchen: "Agriculture is our wisest pursuit, because it will, in the end, contribute most to real wealth, good morals, and happiness."

George told his son that one day the farm would be his. "Marc, farming, like any job, is a choice. Mary and I have been very happy here. You are no stranger to its hard work, but you may decide to embrace another profession. Your mother and I will support whatever decision you make."

Even with all the love and support of his adoptive parents and the fullness of his life, Marc knew there was something missing. One Sunday afternoon, he broached the subject of locating Nicole.

"I miss Nicole. She will be thirteen this year. I dream about her and pray that I will see her again."

"Your mother and I were wondering when you might want to talk to us about this. We know you must miss her very much." The three discussed various ideas about how to locate her.

One evening at dinner, Mary told Marc that she wrote a letter to the French Embassy in Washington D.C. "Marc, I gave them Nicole's name, the names of the couple who adopted her, and the town in France, Ibos, where they are living. I told them your history and our part in it. I gave them our contact information. I am hopeful we will get a response from them."

On a Saturday in early September Mary ran into the house with a letter in her hand from the French Embassy. She threw the other mail on the table and ran out to the barn where George and Marc were working on the tractor. She waved the letter at them. "This is from the French Embassy! This could be good news or bad news, so Marc, let's pray for good news!"

Mary carefully opened the envelope and read the letter to Marc and George:

"This is to acknowledge receipt of your letter of August 17, 1947, in reference to a request for information that we may be able to provide regarding the whereabouts of a Monsieur Maxime and Madam Justine Colbert and their adopted daughter, Nicole. As stated in your letter, the Colberts received custody of Nicole from the Orphanage of Saint Stephen located in Tarbes, France. We have been informed that the Orphanage of St. Stephen was shuttered near the close of hostilities with Germany in late 1944 and all records from that institution have been destroyed.

"France is currently under an economic recovery plan and taxes are being collected in most towns and cities throughout the country. We have been notified that a Maxime Colbert is listed on the tax filings for the city of Ibos, France, located in the township of Bordères-sur-l'Échez, part of the district of Tarbes, France. It is suggested that you contact the municipal council for the city of Ibos, as they may be able to provide more specific information regarding your inquiry. The address for the Ibos municipal council is enclosed.

"We will retain your inquiry in our active file, and will convey to you any future information we may acquire concerning this matter. We wish you success in your search."

Mary took a deep breath and looked at Marc. "Well, Marc, this is a hopeful response. We will send a letter to the Ibos council as they suggested. A step forward in our search for Nicole!"

"Mother, thank you! Their response is promising! I pray to the Lord that we can find her."

One evening later that week, Mary composed a letter and Marc translated it. They mailed it from the post office the following day, crossing their fingers and hoping for a quick response.

The months passed, and every day Marc hurried to the mailbox with hope and anticipation, only to be disappointed. Mary followed up with several letters, hoping that the correspondence would prompt a reply, but she had read news articles about the slow and dysfunctional mail service throughout Europe. "We just need to be patient, Marc, and remain optimistic."

Following a beautiful white Christmas, a cold, clear February day found Marc busy at the high school with a pre-season soccer meeting and then his usual farm chores and homework. He strolled out to the mailbox and was flipping through the mail when a neatly written envelope, bearing international postage and addressed to Mary and Marcel Whiteford, caught his eye. Holding the envelope in his good hand, he ran to the house, where he found Mary busy preparing dinner.

"Mom! Look what we received in the mail!" Mary wiped her hands on her apron.

"Oh my goodness! It looks like the letter we have been waiting for!" Marc opened the envelope and quickly scanned the letter. It was written in French and signed by Nicole. "Marc, our prayers have been answered. Please read it to me." They sat down at the table. The letter was dated December 18, 1947.

Dear Marcel,

Maman and Papa received a letter that your maman sent to the Town Council of Ibos. My papa is a member of the Town Council. Thank you, and your maman, for searching for me. The letter did not tell us very much about your new life in Maryland. I would like you to write a long letter that tells me all about what happened to you after we said goodbye at the orphanage on that cold day so may years ago. I can still picture you waving goodbye to me. I am so happy to hear that you are safe and have been adopted. The war took so many lives here in France and I thank the Lord that you were not harmed. I have been legally adopted and my new parents are very loving and have given me a new life, but you are the only real family I have.

I am in secondaire le collège (middle school) and attend the École d' Ibos. We live on a small farm that Papa cares for. My maman is a nurse at the hospital here. We have visited Lourdes several times since the Nazis departed. Just by chance, I discovered several of Maman's paintings among other art work at a store in Lourdes, not far from our bakery. They were sitting on the sidewalk. I know they were hers becaue they had her name and her signature butterfly inked on the back of the canvas. I cried when I saw them, but was so happy I discovered them. My maman purchased all of them. Maybe I could send one to you? The bakery is shuttered but the school we attended has reopened. I still wonder about all the friends we left behind, especially Diop.

I think about you every day. Please come to visit me. The mail here is very slow, so promise to write me often. Wishing you and your family there a very Joyeux Noël (Merry Christmas)!

Je t'aime,
Nicole

"Oh, Marc. What a lovely letter."

"Mom, it has been four years since I last saw her. Do you think we can travel to France? I miss her so much."

"Marc, George and I want very much for you to see your sister. The war has just ended and France is rebuilding. I am not sure, but it may be too soon to travel. Let's write to Nicole and see what she can tell us about visitors to France. I will also check with some of our elected officials to see what they may recommend.

"I know your letter to your sister will be a long one. Your life has turned many pages since you last saw her."

One evening in early spring Marc wanted to discuss with his parents his remembrance of the last conversation he had with Diop. They sat around the dinner table as Mary sliced him a piece of her peanut butter cake, Marc's favorite.

"I know I have told you all about my friend, Diop. The last time I saw him, in March of 1944, we talked about how we would try to reconnect after the war once I was settled somewhere. He told me to write to the pastor at the Church of the Rosary Basilica in Lourdes and to tell him where I am living. Diop was going to contact the pastor and tell him to let Diop know if he ever received a letter from me. The Germans surrendered France in June 1944, so it has been four years, but I still have not written to the pastor. I am going to write tonight. I still carry a very worn address book in my rucksack. I hope the address for the Basilica is there."

One day after school in September, Marc walked into the house and saw an envelope on the kitchen table covered in international postage. The return address was the Basilica of Our Lady of the Rosary. Mary was at the stove.

"I thought you might want to open it." The letter, in French from the pastor, Father Cyril Lemere, was brief. Marc read it silently.

Dear M. Whiteford,

This letter is in reference to your inquiry regarding the whereabouts of one of our former parishioners, Monsieur Diop Medar. I have had other inquiries regarding Monsieur Diop, and I am sad to inform you that recent records compiled and released by the French Ministry of Defense indicate that he was killed while fighting for the French Resistance.

May the peace of the Lord be with him and also with you.
Sincerely,
Father Cyril Lemere
Pastor, Basilique Notre Dame du Rosaire de Lourdes

Marc sat down at the table, dropped the letter, and with his hands over his eyes, began to sob. Mary walked over to him and tried to comfort him. Marc pulled away.

"Death continues to follow me. Diop is dead! Killed by the Nazis! He was part of our family. Maman, Papa, and now Diop. The last time I saw him, he told me he wanted to return to Lourdes and open a bakery, just like the one my parents had. He told me a miracle would happen and we would reunite."

Mary stayed close and touched his arm. "Marc, I am so sorry. The war took so much from you. I can only imagine how this news must hurt your heart. Just know that George and I are here for you and we love you." She paused and smiled.

"When I was a little girl, my mother would say, 'Close your eyes and look inside your heart.' That is where Diop will be, next to your mother and father."

Thirty One
May, 1949

A Visit With Nicole

Marc had kept his promise to Nicole and wrote to her almost every month since her first letter arrived. He did not want to tell her about Diop's death in a letter, but would tell her when they had their first face-to-face visit. Nicole responded in turn with her letters. In every one, she closed by asking, "So Marcel, when will you come to France to visit me?" She told him that France was returning to normal with much construction of roads, highways, and new homes. She suggested that when a trip was finally planned, the reunion should take place in Paris.

On May 6, 1949, George and Mary surprised Marc with an eighteenth birthday party, which included a celebration of his upcoming high school graduation. Marc had decided to pursue an education degree at the Maryland State Teachers College located on a large campus in Towson, Maryland, just eight miles north of Baltimore. After much thought, he had decided that his career goal was to become a high school language teacher and a soccer coach.

Many of his soccer player friends had been invited along with his new girlfriend, Lee. All of the guests assembled on the stone patio next to the barn. After the cake was cut, Marc opened his presents. As he was assembling the gifts on the picnic table, Mary went over to him, and with a broad smile handed him a birthday card.

"Marc, please open this. Besides being for your birthday, this is also an early graduation present." Marc opened the envelope and read a touching birthday message in a large card. He found a smaller envelope taped to the back of the card. He opened it to find two airline tickets which showed the destination as Paris, France. He was speechless.

"Marc, you and I are going to fly to Paris to visit Nicole for ten days at the end of June, just after your graduation!" Everyone in the group clapped their hands and sang "Happy Birthday!"

"Mom, Dad, thank you. This is the best gift ever! This will be our first time on an airplane! I can't wait to tell Nicole. I am so excited." He hugged his parents, reluctant to let go.

Marc and Mary counted down the days as they began to prepare for their trip to France. George had decided that as much as he would have loved to join them, he couldn't leave the farm and the animals, but he could at least drive them to Philadelphia to board the aircraft. George told Marc that the Pan Am aircraft would stop in Gander, Newfoundland and Shannon, Ireland and then fly straight to Paris. It would be a very long flight. "Marc, this will be a trip you will always remember—a reunion with your sister!"

Nicole could not believe that she would be seeing her brother soon. She sent a letter outlining a suggested itinerary, very exact, with things to do on each day and a recommendation for a place to stay, the Hôtel de l' Abbaye in Saint-Germain-des-Prés, close to the Cathédrale Notre-Dame de Paris. Nicole told him that her parents would drive from Ibos to Paris. It would be about an eight-hour drive and having the car would allow them to see much more of Paris. She suggested they take a taxi to the hotel from the airport where she and her family would be waiting for them. She also advised them to exchange their dollars for francs at the airport.

The day for their trip to Paris, Sunday, June 19, 1949, finally arrived. George drove them to the Philadelphia airport and helped unload the suitcases. He kissed them goodbye and handed Marc a camera. "Here, son, take a lot of pictures and please tell your sister that I said hello and that I hope to meet her someday. It would be wonderful if she could someday visit us at the farm."

Their quick flight from Philadelphia to New York left at 6 p.m. The trans-Atlantic flight to Gander, Newfoundland was noisy and very turbulent. Mary held Marc's hand for most of the flight. "I don't think I like airplanes," she whispered. "This frightens me!" Marc adjusted her seatbelt and handed her a small pillow to try to make her comfortable.

"Mom, try to get some sleep." The lights dimmed and many of the passengers were asleep, but not Mary. The prop aircraft landed in Gander, and Marc and Mary found their way to the gate for their next flight to Shannon, Ireland and then to the Paris-Orly Airport. They were told that the total flight time from New York to Paris would be almost twenty-five hours. Throughout the trip, Marc did most of the sleeping and Mary did most of the worrying. Once they were on the ground, Mary reached over and gave Marc a kiss on his cheek.

"This flight was much better than I expected, but I think I still don't like flying." Marc laughed and unsnapped his seatbelt.

"Mom, flying is the way to go. Sailing is fine if you have a month to spare to travel. Let's find our luggage and look for a taxi. I can't believe I am back on French soil!"

"I am so looking forward to meeting Nicole. If I'm this excited to see her, I can only imagine what you must be feeling."

They collected their luggage and hailed a taxi. The driver expertly maneuvered his way through the streets of Paris. Mary and Marc could see, at a distance, several of the iconic sites, including the Eiffel Tower and the Arc de Triomphe. They crossed one of the bridges over the Seine River, then entered a roundabout to exit onto a small, narrow street. The taxi slowed and then stopped in front of the Hôtel de l'Abbaye. The driver removed the two suitcases from the trunk as Mary handed him a few francs. Marc carried the luggage and followed Mary into the spacious lobby.

As they approached the clerk at the front desk, a beautiful young girl with long blonde hair ran down the hall toward them. Marc knew it was Nicole the minute he saw her. He dropped the bags and ran to her. They embraced, laughing and crying all at once. Marc called his mother over.

"Mom, this is Nicole. Nicole, this is my mom, Mary."

"I am so very glad to meet you. Welcome to France!" Nicole said in halting English.

"It's nice to meet you, too," Mary said, and gave Nicole a big hug.

Their time together passed all too quickly. Despite the language barrier—the Colberts speaking very little English and Mary very little French—they had fun and got to know each other well, with the help of Marc and Nicole as interpreters. Nicole was taking English lessons at her school and Marc was very impressed with her English language skills.

Nicole planned each day of their visit. Over breakfast she reviewed their itinerary: Monday the Eiffel Tower, Tuesday a visit to the Louvre and Tuileries Garden, Wednesday a walk to the Notre-Dame Cathedral. All of their time together was laid out in detail with places to go, including some well-known restaurants. Everyone congratulated her on her planning skills. Each day was filled with the sights and sounds of Paris. Marc took pictures of everything to share with George.

One evening Marc and Nicole decided to take a walk along the Seine, just the two of them. They held hands and walked past shops and stores, across bridges and then along the stone walk next to the river. The lamplights came on as the sun set. Nicole asked about Marc's amputated fingers as she examined his hand. He told her about his walk across the Pyrénées with José, Leo, and the two American pilots, Tim and Mark.

"Nicole, I have never experienced such cold. I lost a glove, but never thought I would lose my fingers." He mentioned all of the wonderful people that helped him along the way. "I knew Maman and Papa were watching over us. I prayed for you every night. I heard they were bombing throughout France and I thought you might be injured or worse. I worried about you and thought the Nazi soldiers might billet at your house." Marc gently lifted her hand and kissed her birthmark on her finger.

Nicole's voice wavered. "Your kiss reminds me of our meetings at the orphanage. I heard the airplanes and the bombs but they didn't come close to our farm. Lourdes and Tarbes were not bombed but there were German soldiers all over, fighting the Resistance. Marcel, have you been able to locate Diop? I think he became a soldier for the Resistance?"

Marc saw a welcoming bench under two large trees close to the river bank. "Nicole, let's sit here for a while. The last time I saw Diop was in March of 1944, just before I started my walk across the mountains. We developed a plan so we could reunite after the war. We agreed that we would try to reconnect through the pastor at the Rosary Basilica in Lourdes. Last year I received a letter from the pastor, Father Cyril Lemere, stating that records were released by the French Ministry of Defense indicating that Diop was killed in combat."

"Oh, Marcel, no!" Nicole gasped, and began to cry. She placed her head on her brother's shoulder. "Marcel, he was family. He watched over us and helped so many. I thought I would see him again, too."

"The war took so many, Nicole, and France has suffered. Diop was so young and wanted to open his own boulangerie." Nicole wiped her eyes. "The tragic echoes of war will always surround us but it is the memories of family and friends that we must hold on to."

The brother and sister held hands and gazed out over the Seine, deep in their thoughts about those whom they had loved and lost. Nicole broke the silence.

"So, Monsieur Whiteford, tell me, what are your future plans? You just graduated from secondary school and you told me you will be attending college."

"Yes, I will be attending a college not too far from where we live. I want to be a language teacher at a high school and would like to be a soccer coach as well. I will still be able to help my father with the farm. Oh, and I want to tell you about my girlfriend, Lee. I really like her. She wants to be a primary teacher. The good news is that we will be attending the same college, so we will see each other all the time! Tell me your plans."

"Marcel, my plans are still a bit uncertain and my future remains a question mark. I would like to attend the Centre Universitaire Tarbes Pyrénées and maybe become an art teacher. The university is a short drive from our farm. Our maman encouraged me to paint and I have been creating some water color art. My new family is very supportive of my art. Congratulations on having a girlfriend, Marcel! But no boyfriends for me."

"No?" teased Marc.

"Marcel! I'm only fifteen!" Nicole changed the subject.

"I would like to come visit you, maybe next summer. I can't believe that both of us are living with new parents on a farm. I miss our parents and I will never forget them and their deaths at the hands of the Nazis. The brutality of the war will touch us for as long as we live."

They continued to talk, reminisce, and tell stories of their birth parents. As they walked back to the hotel, they passed an inviting boulangerie with smells they remembered from their childhood. Marc looked at Nicole. "Do you think they may have some of Papa's spiced honey bread?"

Their visit was much too brief and they agreed that Nicole, Max and Justine would visit Marc in Maryland. Marcel took pictures of everyone at their goodbye breakfast at a café they had discovered together on one of their outings. Mary gave Justine, Max, and Nicole wrapped gifts as Marcel asked the waiter to take one last photograph of the group.

Marcel then took his last picture of Nicole as she held her present from Mary. "Nicole, I will be mailing you the photos I took. Thank you, Monsieur Colbert, for being our taxi driver. This has been a wonderful visit with our new extended family. You know it is only thirty-eight hundred miles from Maryland to France, so let's visit often." Everyone laughed and agreed that was not so very far at all.

Marc had a busy four years with college studies, soccer, and farm life. His relationship with Lee grew stronger. They both graduated from college in June of 1953 and were hired as teachers in Harford County, Maryland. Together they achieved their career goals, with Lee teaching second grade and Marc teaching French and English at the high school where he graduated.

After long discussions with their parents, Marc and Lee decided to marry. The wedding was planned for August of 1954 at St. Ignatius Church, where they both attended. George and Mary insisted that Marc and Lee live on the farm. They tore down walls and made other improvements to the old farm house to accommodate them. Marc understood that George still needed his help on the farm, so the arrangement was beneficial to them both. Lee had mentioned to Marc that she always wanted a pony and dogs, so living on the farm with his parents was perfect.

Marc kept the promise he made to Nicole—that he would be a faithful letter writer. With great excitement, he penned a letter to her and told her about the wedding plans. In her response, Nicole told him that she and her mother would travel to Maryland for the wedding. She wanted to meet Lee and spend time at the farm and finally meet Marc's father. Marc read part of her letter again.

Marcel, I am so happy for you. I know your life with Lee will be a happy one. Looking forward to our visit. It has been five years since our Paris reunion! I do want to let you know that I visited a friend in Lourdes just last week and while there I noticed a memorial plaque that has been recently placed on one of the buildings near the church. It lists the names of Lourdes residents who died in the Nazi concentration camps. Our dear maman's name is listed. I took a photograph of the plaque and will mail it to you.

On Saturday, August 14, 1954, St. Ignatius Church was brimming with wedding guests. Flowers and music filled the church. Lee had asked Nicole to join the wedding party as a bridesmaid. Marc told Nicole that, with the exception of his bride, she was the prettiest one there. The nuptial Mass was both joyful and solemn, the smiling guests dabbing their eyes with their handkerchiefs. Following the ceremony, a reception was held at the farm. Mary and George proudly showed Justine around the farm and introduced her to Lee's pony.

Marc and Lee had decided to postpone their honeymoon but would instead spend their wedding night at a beautiful hotel in Baltimore, the Belvedere. Marc lightly packed their car for the quick trip into the city. They found Nicole and Justine about to leave for their trip back to France. Marc and Nicole embraced for a long time, and then Marc held her at arm's length.

"Nicole, this has been the happiest day of my life. I have found the love I have been searching for. I am so blessed that you were a part of this day and will forever be a part of my life. I love you, dear, sweet sister."

*   *   *   *   *

Over the years there were many trans-Atlantic crossings, primarily for family events: Nicole's graduation from the university and then her wedding to Lucas; the birth of Marc and Lee's son, Joseph, and his marriage to Julie; the tragic death of George in an automobile accident; and Mary's death from cancer.

After thirty years of teaching, Marc decided to retire. The farm had always been a big part of Marc's life. Following the deaths of George and Mary, Marc and Lee decided to keep the farm but downsize it. They rented out most of the acreage to farmer friends who planted corn and soy beans. Marc kept some horses and other animals and his chickens.

One evening after dinner, Marc told Lee that he didn't feel well and was having chest pain. "I think I am going to take an aspirin and lie down for a bit." After a short while, he came back down and found Lee in the kitchen. "Lee, I am really not feeling well. I think I should get to the hospital. Let Joseph and Julie know."

Lee drove Marc the thirty minutes to the hospital. At around three in the morning the doctor found Lee praying her rosary in the waiting room. He sat next to her and held her hand. "I am sorry to tell you, Mrs. Whiteford, but your husband has passed. He went into cardiac arrest that resulted in a massive heart attack. I am so sorry."

Epilogue
November 21, 1992

Joseph walks toward the lectern on the altar. He makes the sign of the cross and takes a deep breath as his eyes look upward. "This eulogy will be very difficult for me and maybe the hardest thing I have ever done. Our family thanks you for being with us today to say goodbye to my father, Marcel Whiteford. We were hoping that Dad would enjoy a long retirement, but the Lord had other plans.

"Dad believed that life is a journey of joy, hope, love, and sadness. He not only told us what matters in life, he showed us what matters. He said to me, 'Son, there is this line that runs between your birth date and death date. That line is what matters. It's the line that shows the direction of your life.' Dad's life line is my inspiration. It has guided my life's journey. His life will be my beacon and a beacon to many others who knew and loved him.

"Dad was passionate about his teaching and his soccer teams. I was fortunate to have him as my soccer coach for the four years I played in high school and I see so many of his former students and players here today. For those of you who played for him, you will remember that on the first day of practice he would gather the team together and give an inspirational pep talk. He would tell them about the loss of his fingers to satisfy their curiosity. He would raise his hand and point to where his fingers were amputated. He would say, 'You don't need these to play soccer.' Then he would point to his head, legs, and heart. 'You do need your head, your legs, and your heart. Your heart is where your motivation and love of the game can be found.' He would tell us to work hard in the classroom but harder on the soccer field.

"There may be some here this morning who might not know about my Dad's life as a child in Lourdes, France during World War II. His childhood was surrounded by death and repeated goodbyes. The Nazis killed his father, and his mother later died in a German concentration camp. He and his sister were cared for in orphanages and his sister was adopted by a French family. The Germans began arresting children when it was discovered that they had a Jewish parent.

"A decision was made for him to cross the Pyrénées Mountains, at age thirteen, to safety in Spain. A Spanish guide led him across the snow-covered mountains along with two American airmen and another boy. From there, he made his way to England and then to the United States. He was taken in as a foster child and later adopted by George and Mary Whiteford, my loving grandparents. He lived the rest of his life on Eagles Wings farm.

"Dad was very careful about sharing his life's journey with me. He let me see small fragments of his life, but as he aged, he began to share more of his childhood and the trauma he experienced. One cold winter's evening, when we were enjoying Mom's Sunday dinner, I heard the story of his trek across the Pyrénées to flee the Nazis and the amputation of his fingers due to frostbite and severe gangrene. So often, when he was asked about the loss of his fingers, he would only say that it was a childhood accident and he didn't want to talk about it.

"I remember when I was a nosy teenager I found a small notebook lying on his dresser. I picked it up and started paging through it. When he walked into the room, I quickly closed it and handed it to him. I know I surprised him when I said, 'Dad, I really want to know more about your life during the war. There is so much you haven't told me.'

"My request prompted many conversations with him. During one of our talks, we were seated in his bedroom. He went over to a cabinet and took out a small model ship sitting in a plastic box. It was labeled HMS *AMETHYST*. He explained that it was given to him, in 1944, by one of his doctors who cared for him while he sailed on the *Amethyst* from Spain to England. He handed it to me and said he wanted me to have it. He said it was a small representation of the largesse of so many people he encountered as he made his way to the United States. He also told me about the notebook. When he was in college, for one of his English writing classes he wrote a diary of the horrors of war experienced by his family and his passage across the Pyrénées. He said to me, 'I wrote it, but I don't like to read it.'

"In his own special way, Dad was my war hero. So many strangers touched his life, saved him, and brought him to the United States, and eventually he found that loving home he was searching for in Harford County, Maryland.

"Dad would often repeat the words of St. Augustine: 'The dead are not present but they are not absent. Our memories keep them with us.' Dad, we may not have the joy of seeing you, but we know that we will always remember you and we know you watch over us. Your life has inspired us. I love you and you will never be forgotten."

THE END

FAMILY:
WHERE LIFE BEGINS
&
LOVE NEVER ENDS

Acknowledgements

A very warm thank you to my dear family for their love and support. Also, thanks to those who reviewed the draft text and provided comments and recommendations.

I would like to send a special thanks to Brenda Haupt for her editing, inspiration and advice.

Historical Fiction

Now We Are Orphans-WWII Escape from Nazi Terror: A Story of Horror, Hope and Family Love, is a work of historical fiction. Many of the locations, incidents, dialogue, and characters (with the exception of well-known historical and public figures) are products of the author's imagination and are used fictitiously. Events are built around a historical context, but are fictional.

About the Author

J.R. Miller was born in Baltimore, Maryland, where he attended the University of Baltimore and received a Bachelor of Science degree in Finance. He also holds a Master's degree in Governmental Administration from the Fels School at the University of Pennsylvania. He held executive positions in governmental procurement and was an instructor and consultant for NIGP: The Institute for Public Procurement. He has authored textbooks and taught procurement, management and leadership classes throughout the United States and Canada. Additionally, he was an adjunct professor at Harford Community College in Maryland and the University of Virginia.

References/Acknowledgements and Inspirational Attribution

War and Remembrance by Herman Wouk
Kristin Hannah-various novels
Alan Furst-various novels
Daniel Silva-various novels
The following web sources were used to
determine historical accuracy:
www.historynet.com/world-war-ii/Auschwitz
www.wikipedia.org/National_Front-French-Resistance
www.theholocaustexplained.org/the-camps/ss-concentration
www.wikipedia.org/Pat_OLeary_line
www.catholiceducation.org/en/culture/history
www.smithsonianmag.com/history/orphanage
www.bing.com/
search?q=english+to+french+translation&form
www.thenation.com/article/archive/innocents-lost

Printed in the United States
by Baker & Taylor Publisher Services